Sexual Jeopardy

A novel

By
Richard Jeanty

RJ Publications, LLC

Newark, New Jersey

To Erica, much Blessings!

1

The characters and events in this book are fictitious. Any resemblance to actual persons, living or dead, is purely coincidental.

RJ Publications
richjeanty@yahoo.com
www.rjpublications.com
Copyright © 2008 by Richard Jeanty
All Rights Reserved
ISBN 0976927780

Printed in Canada

February 2008

1-2-3-4-5-6-7-8-9-10

Acknowledgements

First, I would like to give thanks to my beautiful daughter for being a part of my life. You motivate me everyday and I enjoy every passing moment with you. Special thanks to Stacey for giving me the most beautiful child. I would like to thank my dad for his continued support and for spreading the word about my books. I appreciate everything that you have done and I'm always glad to make you proud.

A big shout-out goes out to all my brothers and sisters and my nephews and nieces.

I'd like to thank all the people who started with me who are no longer reachable because of time constraint. Thanks to all my friends who continue to show interest in my work. I would also like to thank my editor Nance Rousseau.

Last but not least, I'd like to thank all the folks who have supported me through the years: the book clubs, my fellow authors, the readers, bookstores, street vendors and reviewers.

Introduction

Most of us go about our daily lives without a clue as to what's going on in the world. For some, they live a hard life and only leave their hopes in the hand of the Lord, while others appear to be more blessed from birth. The world can be as simple as we make it, but not everything in the world is as simple as it appears.

I chose to address the subjects of AIDS in this book because I no longer want to remain silent about a subject that has been so devastating specifically to the African race. Whether facts or fiction, I hope to challenge your knowledge as well as your vulnerability regarding HIV and AIDS.

The majority of Africa has suffered the brunt of this devastation while propaganda to deflect the true origin of this disease has spread around the world. It's always so easy to take advantage of people's ignorance and lack of education, but not all of us have become so ignorant that we won't take the time to question what's going on in the world.

I'm only hoping to open your mind and broaden the spectrum of the reality that we have been dealt regarding HIV and AIDS. I don't want to convince anybody of anything, but I do hope that you look at the other side.

As always, thanks for your support and time.

Chapter 1
My Story

I don't know what the hell I got myself into, but I almost ruined my life because of my sexual urges and nonchalant attitude about life. Normalcy for me for the last four years was football practice, schoolwork and girls. Oh, yes, the women...I couldn't live without having at least two or three in my room a week. The motel called "Chez Ron" was open for business from eight o'clock until dawn. Any woman who walked through my dorm room was either getting served or serving me. I played no games when it came to booty. I was the Mack of all Macks and the ladies showed their appreciation by turning my dorm room into a revolving door for sexual gratification. The list went on and on and on: Cheryl, Tanisha, Carmen, Rosa, Carolyn, Marsha, and every other name in the book that was available to me. Ethnicity played no role when it came to my satisfaction. No woman gave me a better blowjob than Marsha, a white girl from Suffolk County, Long Island. Kim Chow was my "me so horny" Asian chick who let me hit it all night long. Rosa was my crazy Puerto Rican chick who brought me "Arroz con Pollo" whenever my stomach was too empty for sex. And Cheryl was the bomb diggity chick from Brooklyn, whose tight pussy was out of this world.

The all-night sexual romps were what made college so much fun for me. A lot of guys think that college is not fun because of all the hard work associated with graduation, but I beg to differ. As long as a person is focused college can be the most fun experience. Let's face it, hard work doesn't go away even after a person has graduated from college. If a person is driven, he's going to continue to work hard throughout his life to achieve his goals, and I'm exactly that person. While sleeping with a lot of women was fun, I was not gonna let pussy ruin or dictate what I did with my life. Well, the ruining part I later found out was something that I was too careless to control. Honestly, I can understand how a man can allow a nice piece of ass to take him away from his focus if he's a weakling.

I'll use Cheryl as the perfect example. That chick could've easily been my demise when I was in college. I mean, the things that she did too me sexually was unbelievable. I met her during my freshman year in college and I never stopped fucking her until she dropped out after getting pregnant by one of the basketball players. Cheryl was gorgeous and had a body that I could never get enough of. Her lips were the most satisfying asset she possessed. I remember the first time I received my first kiss from Cheryl it was heaven. Her full lips were entangled in mine and being young and impressionable, I thought they were paradise. She was an experienced sophomore who saw me as the Denzel of campus for some reason. The day she kissed me was the day that my reputation as a ladies' man began. Every female on campus was curious about me because Cheryl didn't hide the fact that she was digging me.

A week after we met, I found myself in Cheryl's single dorm room completely naked, kneeling in front of her, eating her out like she was my breakfast, lunch *and* dinner. The acrobatic split of her legs while she sat in her chair exposed the pinkness of her pussy and I was mesmerized. Her clit was longer than usual and my tongue couldn't get enough of it. I licked and she moaned; and I licked and she moaned. Just the position she was in alone had my dick standing straight up in the air waiting for penetration. I always knew that eating a woman right was the way to her pussy, so I continued to eat Cheryl. Every time I hardened my tongue and stuck it inside her, she started trembling. I figured she enjoyed oral, but she was more of a penetration freak. Therefore, I continued to tongue fuck her while my finger massaged her clit. Soon, my head was in a chokehold at her mercy and she was screaming, "I want you to fuck me!" Of course, I obliged. After wrapping myself in an extra large condom, I turned Cheryl around to kneel on the chair while holding the back of the chair for support. Her ass was completely open to me and I slowly inserted my dick into her. Her pussy was nice and tight and kept the warmth around my dick to a perfect temperature. With ease, I started stroking her slowly. "Oh, your dick feels so sweet," she cooed to satisfy my ego.

I had never had the freedom of sexing a woman without worrying about getting caught by my mom or dad, so I enjoyed tearing Cheryl's ass to shreds after realizing that nobody would come barging through the door. It was nothing but straight sex as Cheryl and I ended up on her single bed with me on top of her as she lay on her stomach. She loved taking it from behind and I enjoyed giving it to her. As I held on to her waist, banging her as hard as I could, Cheryl started screaming, "I'm about to cum. Keep fucking me hard." I accelerated the speed of my strokes and soon I heard, "I'm cumming! I'm cumming!" I wasn't too far behind her, as I let out a loud roar with enough protein exiting my penis to help an anorexic back to normal weight. That was four years ago

7

in college. Things are a little different now that I've graduated.

Chapter 2
The Beginning

My name is Ronald Murphy. I am 33 and I have a story to tell that will change your life. My life was very easy going until I met the baddest woman I ever saw in my life. I want to tell you about the drama I went through.

Being a moderately handsome, charismatic and intelligent man has made it easy for me to talk to the opposite sex. Ever since I was in college, the ladies adored me. The fact that most women find me charming probably contributed to my confidence with women. In college, I played football as a running back. I was not a superstar on the football field, but I excelled in the classroom. For some reason, people always thought it was something amazing that I was articulate as a college athlete. To be honest, I never really liked sports as much as I liked women. However, I discovered that I was able to get a lot more women because of sports very early on in my life. Women just love themselves some athletes.

My daddy, George, always wanted to be a basketball player when he was young, but he did not have the opportunity to play because he had to work a part-time job after school to help support his family. My dad was naturally strong and had the ferocity of a lion. I inherited most of his physical attributes except his height. My dad is a big tall man who stands about six feet four inches tall and weighs about 240 pounds. In college, I weighed about 190 pounds standing at five feet nine inches tall. I was not top- or bottom-heavy. My weight was evenly distributed. I wasn't one of those guys with a big chest and arms standing on pencil legs. I'm very muscular all

9

over. I have seen many of those guys in my days and I always wondered why they never worked on their legs.

From the time that I was in my junior year of high school girls have been telling me how handsome I am. Armed with this knowledge, I never had any self-esteem issues. I'm not arrogant, but I'm very confident. Most people think I am as handsome as my father, but when they see me with my mother, they say that I favor her more. My mother, Alice, is a beautiful dark-skinned woman with long curly hair and she can still turn a few heads in her late fifties. My dad is also a good-looking man, but I think most of my physical beauty came from my mom. My parents have the same dark complexion and I came out as dark as they wanted me to be. People say that I have an infectious grin and my big brown eyes just make the opposite sex melt. I have heard it all from women. Some women are ignorant enough to like me just because they think I have "nice hair." Sometimes, I find some of these women pathetic because my hair has nothing to do with my personality. I feel that Black people need to grow out of that "nice hair and light skin" stigma, but we'll get to that.

I inherited my father's tree-trunk legs and his natural strength. I graduated with honors in high school coupled with my athletic achievements. I was the top running back in the city of New York, but I wasn't heavily recruited because of the division I played in. Hofstra University was the only school that offered me an academic scholarship. I never wanted to go to school on a football scholarship because I did not want any added pressure on me. However, I changed my mind about playing football very quickly after I attended a college

party while visiting the university when I was in my
senior year of high school. It was a party hosted by the
football players; there were more women there than I had
ever seen in my entire life; and most of them were
throwing themselves at the football players. Everyone
had a groupie whether he was a starting player or a bench
warmer. I realized being an athlete had its benefits and I
wanted to get the perks. Since the coach already knew
my skills and abilities in high school, it was almost
automatic that I was going to make the team. I became
the second string running back on the team as a freshman
and the coach sometimes used me on special teams play
to return punts.

I went through four years of college playing football
primarily because I wanted to sleep with as many women
as possible. I never had dreams of becoming a
professional athlete. Football was a recreational sport
that my dad got me playing to keep me out of trouble; I
got used to playing it; and my dad enjoyed watching me
play. I am sure if I dedicated, as much time to football as
I did to the ladies, I could have been a professional.
However, I never had those ambitions. It seems like I
always had only two ambitions in life: to have many
women and to own a nightclub.

In school, my primary focus was always academics
because I was a business major. As a business major, I
had some tough classes and realizing my dream of
owning a nightclub with my dad was the goal. My dad
had worked as a nightclub manager all his life, but he
never owned anything other than his house. I wanted to
get a piece of the pie and I wanted my dad to be part of
it. With my business background and my dad's expertise

11

in nightclub management, it would be a win-win situation and combination. After securing a part-time job as an assistant manager at a local nightclub located near my campus when I was a junior in college, I discovered that I really like the club environment and I dedicated myself to owning my own club. I was offered a full-time management job by the same nightclub upon graduation, and it was there that I developed my communication skills as well as my customer service skills.

While working at the nightclub, I tried my best to absorb as much as I could about the business. I learned about special events planning, contests, special parties and packing the place up at least four nights a week and how to run a nightclub, over-all. I worked diligently to educate myself on every aspect of the business and after four years of working for a great man, who tried his best to teach me everything I could absorb in that span of time, I was ready to move on. The day I turned in my resignation was a shock to everyone. I was being prepped to become the general manger for the nightclub because business was booming under my leadership. However, I saw the bigger picture. Why would I want to be a general manager when I could be an owner? I took my expertise with me, the small business loan that I received from the government along with my father's savings and my own personal savings and bought The Heat in Manhattan.

Owning my own nightclub was the first step to financial security. During my first year of business, we netted about half of a million dollars. The money was almost six times the amount of money that my dad earned annually when he was working as a manager. I was happy to see that my plan did not fail and my father never regretted leaving his secured position to become my business partner. When I first approached my dad about my business proposal, he was apprehensive, but with a little reassurance from my mother, he was convinced in no time. I could always count on mom to have my back in everything that I did. Having been a teacher for years in the New York public school system, my mother knew what it was like for a young man to dream big. She had seen quite a few of her former students grow up to be big name rappers and entrepreneurs even when no one other than her believed in them.

My mother was totally opposite of my father. She was never afraid to take risks and she always reinforced the fact that my brother and I should always dream. And not just small dreams either. My mother truly believed that her children could have been anything that we wanted to be. My dad was always wrapped up in his family's security. He was a good provider who bought the family a home when he married my mother after high school. They started out in the Flatbush section of Brooklyn in a run down three-family brownstone home that my dad renovated himself. He would come home from work after a long tiring night and would get a few hours of sleep before waking up early in the morning to go work his regular job as a construction worker then come home to work an additional four to six hours fixing his own home. That three-family brownstone home is now worth close to $800,000.

My mother loves that man for good reasons. He's never turned his back on his family and he made sure that we never went without. When my mother told my dad that she wanted to go back to school to become a teacher, he encouraged her. He held down the house and watched my brother and me so my mother could pursue her dream. By the time my brother and I were ready for kindergarten, my mother had graduated from college and was offered her first job as a teacher at an elementary school in Brooklyn. As children, my brother and I spent a lot of time with our parents. My mother was always the educator who made sure that we read more books than we cared to read. My dad made sure that we were men who knew how to work with our hands as well as our brain. He taught us to stand for ourselves and to always place family first.

As a kid, I can't recall my father having too many friends. He was always home with his family when he was not working. We didn't see too much of our extended family because they lived in Boston. A typical family weekend at my house consisted of an early family breakfast with my mom, dad and my brother; maybe a long drive to the farmers' market for grocery shopping; some household fixing with my dad while my mom did the laundry; a night treat at the movies once a month on Saturday before my dad went off to the nightclub to work and dinner at our favorite Chinese restaurant or Pizza Hut. Saturday was my mother's day off in the kitchen. My dad did not want her to cook anything. My mother insisted on cooking dinner during the week when she got home from work because she wanted to make sure that the family ate dinner together. Family time became a tradition and we grew very close as a result.

I love watching my parents interact with each other. The amount of love that they have between them is enough to infect a whole nation. When I was kid, I wished that I could one day have the kind of relationship that my parents have. It's not as if they never had any quarrels, but they never allowed anything to escalate to the point where they would not speak to each other for more than a few hours. My dad had developed his own system to deal with my mother just as she had developed hers to deal with him.

Whenever they were mad at each other, they took it out on the house. My mother would clean the house spotless and my dad would fix everything that is broken in the house. Therefore, being mad at each other sometimes had its rewards. In addition, my brother and I were always sent to our rooms to read a book. No matter what we did, the punishment was always to read a book. I guess that is why my brother is now a well-known published author with two books under his belt. His first novel was well received by the public and his sophomore effort is slowly becoming a best-seller.

My brother, Ricky and I are very close. He is more creative than I in many ways and his focus was always writing. From the time we were children, he was into James Baldwin, Alice Walker, W.E Dubois and Alex Haley. My brother graduated summa cum laude at Columbia University. He has never been much into sports. He is medium height and slender and has a very sarcastic streak when he wants to be an ass. There is always more than meets the eye with him. He has always been more analytical than the rest of the family. He has never accepted what's on the surface.

Ricky and I are only two years apart, but he is mature in ways that I can only wish that I could be. He has followed the same path as my parents regarding relationships. He has been with the same woman for the last ten years. Ricky married his college sweetheart right after college and they have been happily married ever since. He is a good looking, intelligent guy who could have probably slept with just as many women as me or even more if he wanted to, but he has always been focused. My brother has always known what he wanted to do with his life and I admire that about him. Sometimes I am even a little envious. That's my older brother.

After he received his bachelor's degree in English from Columbia, he went to New York University to pursue a master's degree in creative writing. His wife Tanya knew that she had a gem in him and she knew that she wanted to hold on to him a week after they met. I love the fact that my brother has only been in love with one woman and he does not have to juggle a bunch of women like I do. My brother is truly my hero, but what I love most about him is that he is nonjudgmental. He has never once judged me for what I have been doing. I knew he always wanted to settle down and focus as he has done, but he also recognized that we are very different people cut from the same cloth. I love my brother.

Chapter 3
If Looks Could Kill

I met Shauna in July 1994 while I was on vacation in Miami during independence weekend. My friend Myles and I decided to fly down to Miami to relax in South Beach, Florida for a few days. We went down with no expectations. We simply wanted to go down there to ease our minds from the crazy life in New York City. We never anticipated meeting two of the most gorgeous women that the world has to offer.

We left the hotel early that morning after eating the free continental breakfast that was offered. We knew everything in South Beach was expensive, so we had planned to make the best of our free meals at the hotel everyday. We did not go to South Beach to waste money, we went there to relax and have a good time. Myles and I shared a room with two double beds for economics sake. We both had just graduated from college and we didn't really have too much money to throw around. I had a great job waiting for me at the nightclub where I had been working part-time for the past couple of years, but I could not start working full-time until after the independence weekend.

Myles had just graduated from New York University with a degree in computer engineering. He was also waiting to start his new position with an engineering firm in New York City when we got back from our mini vacation. We had wanted to get away for as little money as possible and Miami was the cheapest vacation package we found. We arrived in Miami on Thursday night and we were scheduled to leave on Monday so we could report to our new jobs on Tuesday. My mom and dad had given me some spending money as a graduation gift for my vacation. Myles's parents had also given him his spending money.

Each of us had about $300 to spend. We had a very simple plan for our vacation; we wanted to spend all day at the beach; eat a light lunch everyday at one of the cheapest eateries on Ocean Avenue; and at night eat dinner at some of the most affordable restaurants we could find. There was no room for splurging. At night, we would try to frequent the clubs that offered free admission so that we would not run out of money before our vacation ended. We had a budget of about $60 a day. We both had our credit cards in our wallets as back up in case we ran out of money, however it was understood that we had a spending limit.

Since it was our first morning in South Beach, we wore our bathing shorts and tank tops to the beach. We were halfway out the door, when we both realized how crusty and ashy our legs and arms looked. We each had brought a special bottle of baby oil to rub on our bodies to display all of our hard work in the gym and we almost forgot to use it. Myles was my workout partner in the gym back home. We were both very muscular and toned and we knew that the baby oil rubbed all over our bodies would make us look like professional exotic dancers on the beach. *Who the hell wants to look like a male stripper?* Looking like a male stripper beats looking ashy any day. After realizing that we looked like we had already spent time on the beach by the amount of ash that was showing our skin, we took five minutes to rub oil all over our bodies. We each grabbed our sunglasses and threw a couple of towels over our shoulders.

We stepped out of the hotel looking like Mr. Clean with our shiny baldheads. I could only see the back of Myles's head as he was a few inches taller than I, standing at six feet, two inches. He was joking about the fact that the glare on the top of my dome could cause someone to go blind. Myles had his moments with the jokes, but I had my own as well. He looked like a building standing on two posts. We both worked on our legs relentlessly in the gym, but Myles could never get his chicken legs to grow with the rest of his body. After he made his comment about my dome, I turned to him and said, "I saw a gang of chickens walking down the street looking for you. When I asked them what they wanted from you, they told me they wanted to get their legs back from you because chicken legs don't look right on humans." Myles started laughing because he knew that I had let this joke marinate over time before I unleashed it on him. He gave me a big dap and said, "That was a good one."

We had been lying out in the sun on the beach for close to two hours and it was getting boring. We wanted to walk over to the Kenneth Cole store that we noticed the night before when the cab dropped us off at our hotel. I have always been a fan of Kenneth Cole fashion and I wanted to browse a little even though I did not plan to buy anything. Myles did not mind taking the walk with me. However, he was more a Ralph Lauren/Polo guy.

Myles and I were crossing the street to go to the Kenneth Cole store located a block up the street on Collins Avenue when it all happened. As we crossed halfway into the middle of the street, two goddesses driving a silver convertible Mustang GT appeared out of nowhere. For a moment, we were both lost in the women's beauty. We forgot we were standing in the middle of Ocean Avenue with a bunch of impatient motorists honking their horns at the convertible Mustang telling them to move it, not realizing that Myles and I were blocking their way. We slowly moved out of the way to see the women drive by us almost in slow motion so we could get a better look at them.

We thought we had caused a small commotion by holding up traffic, but we soon realized that all eyes were on the two women sitting behind the wheel of the convertible Mustang. All that I could say excitedly to Myles was "Did you see that!" He turned to me and the look on his face said it all. We knew that we had seen the two most beautiful women that we had ever laid eyes on. It took us about a minute to allow the two women to fade away in traffic before we turned around to head to our original destination.

We found it strange that we didn't even say anything to the ladies as they drove by us. It was almost as we were caught in a trance and we *couldn't* say anything. They didn't bother to speak to us either. As Myles and I walked up the side street to the store, we were talking all kinds of crazy shit about the ladies. We were saying things like "they know they're fine and they're probably money hungry and hoping to score with the next big professional athlete on South Beach." We went on and on about them until we noticed they were pulling around the corner headed towards us again. They had apparently driven around the block and we must've caught their attention during our little stunt while crossing the street earlier.

This time, I was ready to say something as the ladies drove by us. As we started to step onto the street to start crossing before them again, we noticed that they both tilted their sunglasses to give us a look of interest. I immediately took advantage of their interest and asked them to pull over for a few minutes. The light-skinned girl was in the passenger seat while the dark-skinned girl was driving. Myles and I never had any disagreements on the type of women we liked and the type of women who were attracted to us. Because I am dark-skinned, I found it easier to talk to the light-skinned women. They were almost more approachable to me and they often found me more attractive than dark-skinned women. It's that "opposites attract" theory. Don't get me wrong, I think my mother is the most beautiful woman on this earth. She looks just like Cheryl Lee Ralph. I just have never met any dark-skinned women who were not looking to date someone lighter than they were. That was just my experience.

Ever since I was a kid, I found it hard to talk to the women who shared my complexion. Most of them sometimes looked to the light-skinned pretty boys for help with their self-esteem issues. It almost seemed like their self-hatred is so deeply rooted that if they could somehow dilute their bloodline with a light-skinned man everything would be all right. The same could be said about many dark-skinned brothers as well. Personally, the first thing I notice about a woman is her smile, body, ass and intelligence. Complexion has never been a factor.

21

However, the colonial mentality is still alive and well with a lot of brothers and sisters today.

I once dated a dark-skinned woman who told me that I wasn't her usual type. When I enquired about what her usual type was, she told me that she usually went out with tall light-skinned men with green eyes, as if I was supposed to be flattered by her ignorant ass comment. I left her ignorant ass sitting at the restaurant after she made that ignorant statement. Sometimes you have to fight ignorance with ignorance. My ignorant ass felt good leaving her ass sitting in the restaurant not knowing whether I was coming back. And I never went back.

My own mother and father have called me prejudice because I seldom brought home a dark-skinned woman. What they never understood is that these women never want to give me the time of day. I have tried so many times to talk to dark-skinned sisters and each time they tend to gravitate towards Myles. Like I said, Myles and I always knew the score and the dark-skinned sister behind the wheel had a big Kool-Aid smile on her face when she saw that Myles was headed to the driver's side of the car after they pulled over near the curb. She was gorgeous and fine at the same time. She had beautiful dark skin with shoulder length hair, cut in a bob style. From the way she was sitting in that leather seat, her thighs left the impression that her booty had the perfect dimension that men crave from a sister.

The light-skinned woman on the passenger side was not only fine and gorgeous, but she was also extravagant. She was very natural with flawless skin and the sexiest red lips that I had ever seen. She wore her hair short in that style Anita Baker made famous during the late eighties. My eyes didn't even get a chance to travel all the way down her thighs, because I had to stop at her double D cups for a few minutes before I could regain my composure. They were both wearing their two-piece bikini bathing suits with a see-through skirt wrapped around their waists. Before we could start making small talk with them, we started taking inventory of their beauty and bodies. Myles and I could not believe our eyes. These women were as fine as God could make women.

I introduced myself as Ronnie to the light-skinned one and she reached out and firmly shook my hand as she told me her name was Shauna. I responded, "A beautiful name for a beautiful lady." I pointed over to Myles and I told her "that's my boy, Myles." She pointed to her friend sitting next to her and she told me "that's my girl, Chenille." Shauna and Chenille looked good enough to eat and we were hungry. Since we hadn't eaten lunch, I decided to invite the ladies to have lunch with us. That whole budget plan we had for five days was about to be thrown out the window. Myles knew that in order to spend any time with these ladies we were going to have wine and dine them. Women like that didn't just chill with a man for company.

Surprisingly, the ladies told us that they had eaten a huge breakfast and wanted to hold off on eating until dinner because they were watching their weight. So were we and the weight was distributed in all the right places. They suggested that we go lay out on the beach. They asked us to hop in the car so they could go around looking for a parking space. We jumped in the car and they drove back towards Ocean Avenue. As we pulled up around the corner on Ocean Avenue, we noticed this woman pulling out of a spot. I pointed it out to Chenille and told her to take it. However, before Chenille could pull into the spot this big muscular dude walked over and stood there claiming that he was holding it for his friend. I was thinking to myself "This steroid looking white dude is about to get his ass whipped over a parking space." I turned to Myles and I could see by the look on his face that he was down to put a beat down on the man if it came to that.

Myles and I usually do not like to start any trouble with people, but if it found us, we usually dealt with it. We wanted to wait to see how the ladies were going to react to the man's hostile approach to the parking space. We allowed them to talk to the man first. Shauna was closer to him, so she spoke "we've been going around in circles for about a half hour and we pulled up next to the car before you even got there. Is it possible for us to have the space?" With his chest pumped out to the street, that asshole laughed in her face and told her he was not going anywhere and that the space belonged to him. The steroids must've been going through his brain because he was overly cocky for a man who did not know anything about Myles and me.

We told the girls to wait a minute as we jumped out of the car. Myles is taller and a little bigger than I am, so he jumped out the car first. When that asshole took one look at Myles's bicep, he realized that he could be lying on his back quicker than Mike Tyson knocked out Michael Spinks. He decided to move out of the way and took some of the air out his chest so the girls could park. As the girls were parking, his friend pulled up and I decided to jump out the car for assurance. His friend took a look at Myles and me and told him there was a space down the street to hurry back in the car. With that little problem solved, the girls knew that they were not about to hang out with two chumps. That little episode secured our position with the ladies for the rest of our vacation.

After the car was parked, we fed the meter for a couple of hours. Shauna stepped out of the car and for the first time I got to see her total beauty. She stood about five feet ten inches tall, which was taller than I was and her body was a killer. She could not be bigger than a size six and her well-manicured toes were screaming to be sucked. Her body dimensions were perfect in every way. Her bathing suit was a bright fluorescent green color and the see-through fluorescent sarong was tightly wrapped around her waist like a fitted skirt showing her assets to the world. She was even-toned all around and her stomach was as flat as an ironing board. Shauna also had long killer legs that were smoothly shaven exposing her calf muscles.

Chenille was just as fine, but she was about five feet six inches tall with enough junk in her trunk to supply all the junkyards in the entire city of Miami. She was wearing a bright orange bathing suit that complemented her dark complexion. Her sarong see-through skirt was sitting on top of her ass barely making its way below her ass cheeks. We were with two of the finest women that Miami had to offer and it felt great. There was a big disparity in our heights. In a normal situation, Myles should have been with Shauna because they were both tall and light-skinned and looked like they could be a

25

couple. Chenille and I complemented each other a little bit more because I was a few inches taller than she was. However, she was not interested in me and I could tell. It did not make much of a difference to me because they were both beautiful.

We walked across the street to the store to get four bottles of spring water. While we were in the store, we also picked up a few power bars in case we got the munchies. Lunch was a distant worry about this time. After we left the store, Myles and I allowed the women to walk ahead of us so we could get a better view of their behinds. We were giving each other secret handshakes like we had just scored a three-point shot in an NCAA championship game as we watched the women strut in front of us. We couldn't believe how fine these women were and how lucky we were to be hooking up with them. We had banged some bad chicks in our lives, but none of them were as fine as Shauna and Chenille.

As we approached the end of the curb to cross the street to the beach, the ladies playfully told us, "it's our turn to check out the view and y'all need to walk ahead of us." They knew that we had been checking them out from behind the whole time. We had never been put in that situation before and it felt somewhat weird that these women were looking at us, as though we were pieces of meat. We were trying our best to walk sexy and gangster at the same time. We messed the whole thing up and the girls were laughing their asses off. We realized how down to earth they were and we knew that we were going to have a good time with them. We also found out on that day how women feel when men gaze at them like they're on display at the butcher shop. We felt cheap.

Chapter 4
The Gods Were Watching Us

Before we went to the beach, the girls decided to go back to their car to retrieve their beach bags. They had their suntan lotion, along with their towels and lipsticks. They each were carrying bags that matched their bathing suits. Myles and I started smirking when we got to the beach after the ladies lay down their towels and pulled out their tanning lotion. We knew it was going to be our opportunity to feel their skin and to introduce them to our sensually heated hands. I had been known to give a good rub down or two back in college. I had a fast hand on the football field, but my hands are as slow as they can be on the female body.

Initially, Myles and I did not plan to do much sitting in the sun, but after meeting the ladies, sitting in the sun was not a bad idea. We didn't bring any beach towels with us, so we threw the regular towels we got from the hotel on the hot sand next to the ladies to keep us from burning the skin off our asses. A few minutes after the ladies made themselves comfortable on the beach, they both grabbed their suntan lotion. In unison, Myles and I said, "allow me!" It was somewhat corny, but the ladies found it funny as they both handed us the bottles while they turned over on their backs for a rub down.

We could not believe our eyes. Myles and I were like two kids in a candy store. We were about to rub lotion on the bodies of the two most gorgeous women that we had ever met and they willingly wanted us to do something for free that they probably could have charged many of the men on the beach to do. Of course, I am exaggerating a bit here, but these ladies looked that good. Enough about the ladies' beauty already, right? I would say that too, but I have never been mesmerized like that before.

I took the bottle of suntan lotion and poured a little bit of it in my hand as I allowed my hands to explore Shauna's beautiful body. I started around her shoulder area rubbing the lotion as slowly and sensually as possible. I could tell that she liked the way my hands felt on her body as she directed me to a few spots that she claimed I missed. Her suggestions only confirmed that I had the Midas touch because I knew I didn't miss any spots. I ran my hands on the back of Shauna's neck and I noticed she was trembling a little. I knew that I had found her weak spot. Although she did not say anything, her body language told me everything that I needed to know.

I could tell that Shauna wanted to relax while I rubbed her down with lotion, so I didn't initiate any type of conversation. I looked across at Myles; he had all his thirty-two pearly whites showing as if he was in heaven or something. Chenille must've liked the touch of his hands, because I could hear her moaning very softly as he rubbed down her back. I started making my own path down Shauna's back adding a little pressure to a few spots to release some of the tension. As I kept moving my way to down near her butt, she did not say anything. I stopped for about ten seconds before I could get to the part where her bikini separated her back from her ass. She asked why I stopped and I asked her where she wanted me to go. She boldly told me to slowly go down her ass the same way I did the rest of her body.

Shock is not a strong enough word to describe how I felt when Shauna told me to rub her ass down. I prepped my hand as much as I could. I was trying to do finger exercises as I prepared to run them down her butt gently. I poured just enough lotion in my hands and started a circular movement around the right butt cheek, and let me tell you that her ass felt good. I could tell she liked my hand on it as well. I slowly made my way across the other cheek that was screaming for some attention of its own. The more I rubbed, the more Shauna propped her ass up towards me. I finally palmed both of her ass cheeks like I was about to penetrate her right there on the beach pushing her bikini to the side with my hands. Shauna started moaning and told me that I was making her wet. I was thinking "already?" I knew after that comment I was gonna get some ass from Shauna. It may not have been the same day, but eventually. I was hoping for sooner because I knew I was in for a treat.

Shauna's ass felt so good, I didn't realize that I had been rubbing it for almost fifteen minutes, neglecting the rest of her body. She sarcastically asked me if I was going to give her legs some of that rub down love. I had no choice but to oblige. I ran my hands between her thighs and up and down her legs like she was my woman and I was preparing her for some good loving. Shauna welcomed my every move and I just wanted to make sure that her friend, Chenille, was on the same page with Myles. I looked over and Myles gave me the thumbs-up.

After rubbing Shauna's backside down for close to a half hour, it was time to turn her over so I could give her a frontal rubdown. While I was rubbing her ass down, I applied enough pressure to my dick with my legs so that

I control my little friend from rising to the sun. However, facing her beautiful face and bodacious double D cup-sized breasts, made it more difficult for me to keep from getting an erection. After pouring the lotion in my hand, I was contemplating which area of her top I should start working on. I started with her shoulders making my way south near her chest, but her boobs were all over the place and in the way. I did not want to be fresh or risk getting the shit slapped out of me, so I eased my way past her breasts down to her naval. Shauna noticed how I ignored her boobs and said to me "My boobs need some love too." I could not believe what was happening. We were sitting in the middle of South Beach on the sand surrounded by a huge crowd of people and this girl was inviting me to touch her beautiful breasts. I pinched myself to make sure that I was not dreaming.

I can't even recall putting any lotion on my hands, but I rubbed Shauna's tits until her nipples stood erect and my dick could not contain itself in my shorts anymore. My dick was standing like the Eiffel Tower in the middle of Paris on that beach and there was nothing I could do to hide it. At that point, I didn't care how well Myles was getting along with Chenille, I knew that I was gonna be spending most of my vacation with Shauna even if I had to treat her to lunch, breakfast and dinner everyday. Shauna was all I needed to have fun on this vacation.

Thank goodness that I'm well endowed and it showed. I caught Shauna blushing while she stared at my ten-inch tool bulging out of my shorts. I tried to act casual and nonchalant about the whole thing. I knew that Shauna was turned on just as much as I was, but mine was a lot more apparent than hers. I continued to rub lotion down

Shauna's naval and inner thighs until I got down to her ankles. To be honest, when I was rubbing the lotion between Shauna's thighs, I almost wanted to take my tongue and stick it between her legs so I could get a taste of her. I knew that her juices were flowing because her bikini bottoms were a little moist around the entrance of her vagina.

If I had continued to touch Shauna for a minute longer, either I would have exploded in my shorts, or I would have lost my mind. I needed to cool off. I took off running full speed towards the water so nobody could see my manhood standing straight up. I dove in head first and I still could not get my dick to go down after being in the cool water for about five minutes. My mind started wandering and all I could do was think about how I wanted to have sex with Shauna. The more I thought about her, the harder I became. I did not know if Myles took a cue from me, but I saw him running full speed towards the water just like I did a few minutes later. Unless he had a hard-on like me, there was no reason for his mad dash to the water.

Myles finally reached the water and jumped head in first. I could not wait to find out the reason behind his fast relay into the water. After swimming with his head under water for about thirty seconds, he came up for air and found me standing a few feet from him. I didn't want to stay too close to him for fear of violating his space in case he was still hard. It would've looked very funny if two men were standing in the water with their dicks sticking up out of the water. Mine was starting to subside a little and I knew that Myles needed a moment to cool down. I spoke with him from a few feet away. I asked why he rushed to the water the way he did, and by the delay in his response, I knew he had the same experience with Chenille as I did with Shauna.

I swam around for a little while longer to give Myles time to settle down. While I was on my back swimming around and relaxing, Myles came up to me and asked if I thought I was in good with Shauna. I swam back closer to shore where my feet could touch the bottom without drowning so I could have a little conversation with my buddy. In the distance while I was standing in the water talking to Myles, I could see the ladies laughing hysterically. I didn't know whether they were laughing at our situation or not, but whatever it was, it seemed very funny. I didn't really care much about what Shauna thought because I knew that she saw what she had to look forward to.

Chapter 5
Assessing the Situation

One of the first things that I wanted to address with Myles was the fact that we might end up having to treat these ladies for the next five days and our budget was tight. We were trying to figure out a way to pool our money when we go out with them without letting them know. We were also hoping that these ladies would be generous at least once during the trip as well. They were fine, but we weren't gonna be stupid. We definitely weren't willing to foot the bill for everything for these ladies. Myles was miserly with his spending to begin with. We were trying to figure our how this would work because we hadn't had much of a conversation with the ladies. We had done a lot of touching and talking of our own, but we had yet to hear what the ladies wanted to do.

After kicking it for about twenty minutes in the water with Myles, we decided to walk back to the ladies to see what they were up to. They started laughing again as we approached them. I had to ask what the hell was so funny. Shauna took one look at me and said, "The fact that you and your friend are running around on a public beach with your dicks sticking up like kindergarten children. That's what's so funny." I turned to them and said, "Like you all didn't get wet while we were rubbing you down?" By the expressions on their faces and their silence, I knew that my comment was right on target. To ease the situation, Myles turned to us and said, "We all got horny on a public beach, so, what are we gonna do about it?" I was thinking, "No Myles didn't go there." He went there *and* the ladies were fine with it. They wanted to know if we were gonna be hanging out together for the rest of our trip. That shit sounded costly to me, but I knew that most men for the most part, always end up paying for the booty in one way or another. There was no point for us to shop around anymore.

Myles and I sat back down next to the girls for more of a serious conversation. We wanted to know where they were from and why they were in Miami. Shauna told us that she had just graduated from Long Island University and earned a bachelor's degree in business management. She was working for a financial firm and because she had met her department's sales quota, they gave her that Friday off before the long weekend. She decided to take a mini vacation with her best friend, Chenille. They had gotten to Miami the previous night just like Myles and me. Chenille also graduated from LIU, but she studied accounting. She was working as an auditor for Arthur Anderson.

At first, we were trying to have a conversation among the four of us, but a few minutes later, we found ourselves separated as couples and I was only talking to Shauna. Earlier, I had only taken a few glimpses at Shauna's face; I did not really want to stare at her. However, during our conversation, she was sitting so closely across from me that I could almost feel her sweet breath. I looked into Shauna's face and I saw a beautiful flawless woman on the surface. She looked like she was of mixed heritage of either Spanish or White mixed with Black. She had a glow about her that was lively. I could only describe her as a slightly darker and taller version of Selma Hayek.

As Shauna and I gazed into each other's eyes during our conversation, I could tell that she was feeling comfortable with me almost instantly. She kept smiling while listening to me rant about how Myles and I have been friends since high school, how I used to be a good athlete in college and my big dreams of owning my own nightclub one day. She anticipated my excited moments and she encouraged me to speak more. After a few moments of staring into my face, Shauna told me out of the blue that I had nice sexy eyes. It was a surprise compliment, and her touching my hands while she talked was totally unanticipated and welcomed. I found her affection amusing as she divulged more about herself.

Shauna told me that she was originally from the Bronx, she moved to Manhattan with her mother into the Chelsea Housing Projects when she was five years old. She and her dad were estranged. She told me that her mother worked hard to make sure that she made something of herself. Shauna told me that her ambition at one point was to become a publicist, but she gave up on that dream when she realized how hard it was to break into that industry. I was sitting there talking to a woman that I had just met, but everything about her seemed like déjà vu to me. I felt like I had been at the beach with Shauna before and we were a couple in love. She had new dreams of getting her MBA in marketing. Shauna's biggest fear was a roundtrip ticket back to the projects. She had made it out and she never wanted to go back. Shauna's mother at one point neglected her for men, but with the support of family members, her mother was able to regain control of her life and became a psychotherapist.

Everything about Shauna seemed like a fantasy to me. It was as if I was living a dream sitting across from her. I never pegged her to be a down-to-earth person. She surprised the hell out of me. As our conversation lingered on, I also found out that she wasn't so perfect and that was okay. Shauna was highly addicted to high fashion and brand name retail. She would not even think about walking into a Target to buy something as small as lipstick. My high maintenance radar went off like a recess bell in elementary school. She wanted the best of everything and I knew the best of everything cost a lot of money. Since we had established that we were going to spend the rest of our vacation with the ladies, I did not want to appear cheap and changed the plans after Shauna told me about her personal spending habits. I knew I was in for it this time.

Shauna and I also talked about our best friends and how we met them. I told her that Myles and I grew up in the same neighborhood. We played high school football together and that we have always been there for each other. Shauna told me that she met Chenille in college during her first year and they have bonded ever since. Chenille was from a middle class family in Long Island and her parents spoiled her. They decided to become roommates after graduating from college. They lived in the Valley Stream section of Queens.

We had been at the beach for close to two hours and the meter was about to run out. I asked Myles to walk back to the car with me to feed the meter. As we were walking back to the car, I told Myles that this trip was going to be twice as expensive as I expected. I started telling him, though Shauna was down-to-earth in some ways, she was also high maintenance and if I stuck around with her, I'd be broke before I left Florida. He turned to me and said that Chenille was worst because all she kept talking about was a pair of four-hundred-dollar Gucci shoes. "I hope that chick don't think she's gonna get a pair of four-hundred-dollar shoes from me just because she looks good" he said. He continued, "I don't know why she keeps dropping hints like I'ma offer to buy her some shoes and shit. She's out her fucking mind. I might spend a little on dinner and a drink, but she ain't getting no shoes. Her ass is fine, but I ain't paying for it like that."

I just shook my head as Myles went on with his rant because I knew if it came down to us getting some ass from these ladies, we would probably buy shoes for them and more. Not four-hundred-dollar shoes, but some bootleg shoes from Chinatown when we got back to New York. These women were gorgeous beyond belief. Whatever we did, we had to pretend that we were high rollers who could hang with these women for the time being. I told Myles to just follow along as we led these women down a path of deception. I wasn't gonna call them stupid, but if they couldn't put two and two together to figure out that me and Myles were two broke college graduates, that was their problem. We had already told them that we just came out of school. Were they expecting us to have million-dollar jobs waiting back home?

Chapter 6
Planning on a Shoestring Budget

I told Myles not to worry and that I was going to plan everything according to our budgets. My dad once told me, "When people are hungry, the only thing they care about is food, no matter what kind of food it is." My plan was to get these chicks as far away as possible from South Beach at dinnertime. If they were not around expensive restaurants, they could not ask to eat expensive food. I never said that we weren't going to go over our budget, but there was no way I was gonna spend my life savings on a chick I just met.

I appreciated Shauna's honesty about wanting the best in life because she did not grow up with much, but I could not afford to give her the best that life had to offer that weekend on my limited budget. Myles and I casually walked back to the girls after feeding the meter for another hour. We could only get change for a dollar from the place across the street. It was just as well because we had been in the sun for quite some time and a brother definitely did not need a tan. When we got back, we found the girls laughing and giggling like they had no care in the world. I asked, "Are you girls still fantasizing about seeing us naked?" trying to lighten the mood. Chenille answered, "Why fantasize when we have the real thing in front of us?" Now, that's what I was talking about. We were all on the same page. I told the girls that we had an hour left at the beach to chill and after that we could drive around the city to see what was up in Miami. I wanted them to know that South Beach was only a small part of Miami.

The sun was pretty hot and I wanted to stay cool, so I ran back to the water for a quick dip with Myles. I could see the sweat dripping down the girls' gleaming foreheads, but they didn't want to get in the water because they didn't want to mess up their hair. I never understood the deal with Black women going to the beach just to sit around in the sun like they need a tan. The whole point of being on a beach is to enjoy the crystal clear warm water. Myles walked back to the ladies after about ten minutes in the water leaving me alone. He went back to convince them to join us. After much pleading and begging, they agreed to enter the water from the shoulders down. It gave me an opportunity to check out Shauna's erected nipples from the cool water. I know I was not supposed to be looking at Chenille, but her body was banging. Her C-cup breasts were very perky and I could see that she had huge nipples, as they stood erect in her bathing suit top.

We played with the women a little bit while we were in the water without getting their hair wet. After all, they probably would have asked us to pay for them to get their hair done if we had gotten them wet. These women were definitely divas and we had to be on top of our game to deal with them. I could see Myles's big Kool-Aid smile as he wrapped his hands around Chenille's stomach resting his crotch right on top of her round booty. My case was a little different because Shauna was taller than I was. If I wrapped my hand around Shauna's stomach while standing behind her, it would have looked like she had four arms because I would have been hidden from the front due to her height. The fact that she was taller than me, made it a little different for me to get in an intimate position, but she didn't mind. Instead, she stood behind me and wrapped her hands around my chest feeling my muscles.

Overall, we were having a great time with the ladies and they made us feel very comfortable. It was time to leave the beach and we knew that all eyes were on the ladies as we walked back to the car. A man had to be blind not to take a glimpse at them. I saw quite a few women getting upset over their boyfriends' glimpses at our eye candies. We were laughing our asses off as the women berated their boyfriends for looking at the ladies. It seemed like Chenille and Shauna were used to the attention and they knew very well how to deal with it.

We decided to take a drive down to Fort Lauderdale to check out what it was really like in the hood. We wanted to see real people from Florida and how they lived. All those tourists in South Beach could have someone fooled into thinking that the whole city is just one upscale place. After driving around in some of the most depressing neighborhoods in Florida, we realized that some of the Black folks down there really had it bad economically. It was obvious that unemployment was high amongst the Black folks and their run down streets looked like they had not been swept in years by the city's sanitation department. We saw brothers sporting finger waves hairstyles like they were in the fifties. Some were still wearing Jeri Curls and others looked very different from the Black folks in New York all together.

We also drove through Boca Raton to check out some of the more upscale neighborhoods, too. We saw some really beautiful homes, but the cops followed us each time we were spotted by a resident. It seemed like they had strategically stationed police officers in certain corners where we were going to turn. You know they couldn't let us drive through the neighborhood without making sure that our papers were legit.

We were pulled over by two Sheriff Officers without just cause. When I unleashed my knowledge of the law on them, they threatened to lock me up. We didn't violate any laws, but they stopped us for DWB (Driving While Black) in a white neighborhood. Those redneck cops looked like they were ready to pin anything on us, so my whole knowledge of the law was put on the back burner while I pulled out my wallet and gave the officer my license along with everybody else's ID who was in the car. It's not like I didn't know what they did was illegal, but it was too much trouble to fight it at the time. Had I been a Florida resident, I would have seen to it that these cops stopped their racial profiling. I still wrote down their names and badge numbers.

It seemed like "the more things changed in the south, the more they stayed the same" as the old proverb said. I couldn't understand why White people in the south have this deeply rooted hatred and fear of Black people. Their insecurity compromised our safety and rights as citizens. As much as we enjoyed looking at the homes in Boca Raton, we didn't want to give the sheriffs a reason to continue to harass us 1500 miles away from home. It was a good thing that they didn't ask to search the car because they would have had to lock me up before I allowed an illegal search to take place.

For the next couple of days, Myles and I were hanging with the ladies having a great time. They weren't as easy as we first thought. The first day we hung out with them we thought everything as far as us getting some ass from them was pretty much in the bag. However, we found out the hard way that first evening that they were going to tease us for as long as we allowed them. After leaving club Mango the first night with the ladies, we thought we were going to take them back to our rooms and have the best sex of our lives with them, but that all ended with a peck on the lips at their hotel steps.

It was the same thing the second and third night. I don't know if the fact that we did not treat the ladies to any of the expensive restaurants had anything to do with it. We fed them, but not where they wanted to eat. We were always far out as planned when the ladies got hungry and most of the time we settled on eating at restaurants that were nearby when they were dying of hunger. I am not sure if the ladies caught on to our plans or not, but their reactions made it seem like we were being played. At the club, they would be all over us making all the men angry with jealousy and envy. They allowed us to touch them all over and get as freaky as we wanted to be with them, but the minute we got to their hotel, everything ended with a peck on the lips.

Sunday had arrived and it was our last day with the ladies because our flight was leaving early that next morning. Myles and I did not want to spend our Fourth of July in Miami. There were just too many cookouts for us to go to in the City. We did our usual hang out at the beach and drove around the city, but we never offered to take the ladies to any of the restaurants on Ocean Avenue. We only had about $20 left from the $300 that we each took down there with us. We somehow managed to stay close to our budget even though we were hanging with the girls. We went to the clubs where we didn't have to pay a cover charge. Neither of the girls drank, so that saved us a ton of money, too. We bought them a couple of bottles of water and that was it. Myles and I limited our drinking to domestic beers and totally avoided our favorites: Heineken and Corona.

The ladies never had to spend a dime while they were with us. Maybe the ladies were looking for two suckers to finance their little stay in Miami, but we didn't feel like suckers at all, because we were having a great time with them minus the sex. On our last day, we wanted to treat ourselves to a good dinner at one of the fancy restaurants on South Beach and we figured we might as well invite the ladies to join us. The ladies met us at the hotel around six o'clock. When we first saw them, we didn't really recognize them. They had made a transformation that we hadn't seen. They were wearing dresses for the first time since we met them. Shauna was wearing a nice white above the knee loosely fitted linen dress and a nice pair of open-toed white sandals. Chenille looked just as great with her little flowery, cotton body-fitted dress and nice sandals. We all walked over to this nice restaurant on Ocean Avenue for dinner. Myles and I knew that we were about to eat one of the most expensive dinners of our lives and the girls couldn't pass up our offer.

As much as I wanted to sit down and have a nice expensive dinner with my new friends, I also knew that my credit card had a balance of $300 and I had used $100 of it buying pizza at night during my last semester at school. My budget was really $200...no more. We still

43

needed to have enough money to pay a cab to take us to the airport in the morning. As we walked into the restaurant, I gave Myles the look to make sure that he was all right with what we were about do. I did not know if Myles had enough money to cover his share of the bill or not. He nodded to confirm that everything was fine.

We were seated on the front balcony after waiting about twenty minutes for a table. If it were up to Myles and me, we would have been inside eating already. However, the ladies insisted on sitting on the outside balcony so they could be seen. We were about to spend the most money that we ever spent on food, so we didn't mind sitting outside to show off our gorgeous dates. I tried to act like a gentleman and pulled out Shauna's chair for her. Myles did the same for Chenille. The waiter handed us our menus and asked if we wanted start with something to drink. The ladies ordered virgin Piña Coladas while Myles and I ordered Long Island Iced Teas.

I opened my menu first and what I saw almost put a halt to my heart beat. These people had some of the most expensive dishes I had ever seen. It wasn't like we were at a four star restaurant. The main dishes were all forty dollars and up and that was just the chicken dishes. The seafood was almost twice as expensive. And Myles and I knew that the ladies were going to order seafood. It never fails, every time a brother takes a sister out, she always thinks that lobster is the best thing on the menu. Both women screamed out "Ooh…lobster!" We knew what we were in for and we had to budget carefully. I could look at Myles's face and see that he was tabulating everything in his head. I was doing my own tabulation based on the lobster dish that the ladies were about to order.

Being out on a date with a woman I could not afford, on
a budget, was the most stressful thing. I do not know why
Myles and I didn't just spend the last day of our trip
doing our own thing without the ladies. I certainly didn't
want to end up washing dishes in the back of the
restaurant to settle my tab. I did the math in my head and
I figured with the cost of food, tax and gratuity, I had
about $30 left to work with if I ordered the absolute
cheapest dish on the menu for myself. It was better to be
safe than sorry and embarrassed. Myles and I ordered the
cheapest meal on the menu while the girls indulged in the
most expensive dishes. We had to put on an act like we
loved chicken so much that we had to have it. I was
hoping that the ladies didn't want to ruin their appetites
and my budget by ordering an appetizer, but before I
could even finish my thought the waiter was at our table
enquiring whether or not we wanted to start with an
appetizer. I only had a few dollars to work with and I had
no idea what Myles's budget was.

Even the appetizers were close to twenty bucks. They
finally settled on fried calamari as the waiter placed our
drinks on the table. Myles gave me the nod that we were
still within budget and I was relieved. I think the
restaurant industry purposely takes a long time to bring
back people's food so they can force us to order extra
food like appetizers. What the hell is an appetizer,
anyway? Who the hell came up with the idea that we
have to eat something light before we eat the main
course? That is so stupid to me. Most people can't even
finish their main course to begin with. So, why add more
food to the stomach? Anyway, the girls barely gave us a
chance to taste the calamari because they ate most of it. I

was hoping and praying that the waiter did not come back to our table until he was bringing our food. I did not want to order more appetizers. And if we did, Myles and I might as well ask the waiter for aprons because we were going to be scrubbing some dishes.

Luckily, the waiter didn't come back until he brought our food. To be honest, the lobsters looked great and the water in my mouth was running for a piece of it. I could see Myles salivating over it too. I didn't know about Myles, but I damn sure was going to try to get a taste of Shauna's food. My chicken may not have looked as good as Shauna's lobster, but it was just as tasty. When I first dug in my plate for a taste, I was pleasantly surprised how the creamy mushroom sauce over my chicken made it taste like something foreign and better. Although, in the beginning I had planned to act out the whole thing, it turned out that I didn't have to act. My food really tasted great. I offered a taste of my food to Shauna so I could get a taste of hers. After the first bite, she couldn't get enough of my chicken. I liked her lobster too, but my chicken was better.

Myles and Chenille were doing the same thing as we were. They were sharing their food and Chenille couldn't get enough of his. As fine as the ladies looked, these heifers could eat. They almost ate half of our food and all of theirs. I didn't know where the food went, but it was not on their thighs, stomachs or asses. They didn't look like they had an ounce of fat on their bodies. Even after they almost licked their plates clean, they looked like they wanted dessert or something. I crossed my fingers hoping that they didn't have any more room in their stomachs for dessert. I smiled as they sipped on their coladas because I knew the Piña Coladas would fill up whatever empty space that was left in their guts.

By the time the waiter came back to check on us, the ladies had drunk half of their Piña Coladas and they looked like they were uncomfortably full. They had no shame in their game when it came to food and I liked that. I hate taking women out who order food and barely touch it because they think they are too cute to eat. I was waiting for them to start belching since they were so comfortable throwing down like hungry horses in front of us. At that point, I was thinking that a walk was in order. We could not sit at the table to digest our food; we had to be moving. I'm quite sure that Myles and I were not as full as the ladies. We didn't get to eat all of our food like they did.

The waiter did not notice that we were done with everything, I signaled for him to bring the bill to us. I wanted separate bills because I knew that I could not put the whole thing on one card. I told the waiter to put my food and Shauna's on the same bill while Myles and Chenille shared theirs. It would have been too embarrassing if I tried to put the whole thing on my card knowing that I did not have enough money to cover it. It would have been even cheesier if we tried to put one bill on two cards. There was very little room left for error with these women as we were leaving the next day. If we were going to sleep with them, it was going to be that night or never.

After filling our glasses up with water, the waiter handed Myles and I separate bills. I was lucky that mine only came up to $150. I added an additional $20 for the tip. I was guessing that Myles's bill was about the same because we ate the exact same things. I was happy that we did not go over our spending limits. Now, we had to make sure that we spent no more loot because there was no more loot left. I also wanted to try something that we had not tried since we met the girls. I wanted Shauna and me to separate ourselves from Myles and Chenille. I suggested taking a walk with Shauna down on the beach under the moon lit sky.

Chapter 7
Sealing the Deal

At first, Myles could not read the plan, but after batting my eyes a million times and winking at him like I was trying to pick him up at a bar, he finally caught on. I decided to walk down towards the opposite end of the beach with Shauna while Myles and Chenille went in the other direction. I held Shauna's hand as we walked toward the calm waters of South Beach. We saw plenty of people kissing and making out as we strolled down the beach. Shauna and I talked about our future plans and immediate plans when we got back home. I told her that I enjoyed spending every moment with her and that I hoped that our little excursion did not end in Miami. She was game to see me when we got back to New York.

Since I was a kid, my dad used to take me fishing and he would teach me how to skip rocks over water. I wanted to demonstrate my skills to Shauna. I threw a couple of rocks in the water making them skip several times. She wanted to learn how to do it and I tried as best as I could to teach her by holding her hands as intimately as I could to show her the motions. After laughing at Shauna's many failed attempts, she decided to throw her arms around my shoulders and gave me a long wet kiss. It was the first time that I had ever gotten any tongue action from her since we met. Her lips were very soft and sensual and her tongue was warm and smooth. I wanted more of her kisses and she gave me more. Shauna had finally come on board.

I tried to play it cool when she started kissing me. I contained my voracity and my longing appetite for her lips, but Shauna had other plans. She reached for my shirt and started to unbutton my shirt until my nipples were exposed and she was licking on them like I was her dessert. At that point, I really needed some type of back support. So, I led her over to a coconut tree and leaned my back against it while I made out with Shauna. Since it was dark, we did not really pay any attention to our surroundings. We were all that mattered. As I held on to Shauna's body, caressing every inch of her with my hands while I fed my tongue into her mouth with pleasure, I developed this huge bulge in my pants that needed nursing. Shauna could feel my need and she started caressing my crotch as we kissed in the middle of the beach.

She took one of her elongated legs and wrapped it around my body and the coconut tree while she felt me up and kissed me until she got wet enough and whispered in my ear "Let's go back to your room because I want you real bad." I did not need to be convinced. I grabbed Shauna's hand and we rushed back to my room to finish what we started on the beach. Before I closed the door behind us, I hung up the sign that said "Do Not Disturb" on the doorknob in case Myles was trying to come back to the room with Chenille.

I damn near ripped Shauna's dress off after we walked in. Her physique was so perfect I did not need any physical stimulation from her to be turned on. My dick stood up like it was mad at the world at the sight of Shauna's naked body. I pinned her up against the door, started kissing her, and allowed my hands to palm her ass as if it was the perfect basketball. I worked my way down to her breasts and her double D's had my name written all over them. I took her breasts in my mouth one at a time savoring the moment that I had been waiting for all week. Shauna's titties tasted so good I did not want to stop sucking on them. I knew that she enjoyed what I was doing because she kept grabbing my fingers and sticking them inside of her while I sucked on her breasts.

With the urge to satisfy her own needs, Shauna slowly went down to my crotch and took my ten inches in her hands and started stroking it slowly and kissing it all over. I leaned back against the wall waiting for her to take all my ten inches into her mouth to satisfy her hunger and that she did. Shauna started licking me from the base of my balls very slowly and when she got to the head, she wrapped her mouth around it and made her way back down to where she started very slowly while I was completely lost in her mouth. It felt like I died and went to heaven. Shauna sucked me until I could not take it anymore. I tried my best to keep from exploding in her mouth, but I could not resist her technique when she wrapped her hand around the head stroking it back and forth and licking the tip at the same time. I did not know why I felt the need to announce to her and the world that I was cumming, but I could not keep the fact that I was about to bust a nut of great magnitude all to myself. I screamed "I'm cumming, baby! You're making me cum!" And I could see the satisfied look on her face as she looked up at me revealing a devilish smirk.

Shauna spread my semen all over her chest and after squeezing the last drop out, she took me back into her mouth and the shit felt so good my whole body started shaking. "That's what I call busting a nut" I exclaimed loudly. Now, it was my turn to demonstrate my oral

51

skills to Shauna. I had her stand near the desk with one leg up on the chair as I knelt down to eat her like she was a ripe and tasty slice of watermelon. I like the fact that Shauna's clit was long. I took it in my mouth and licked it slowly until it became erect. Her goods were so beautiful and tasty, I could've eaten her for two hours straight without stopping, but Shauna did not want me to eat her for too long as she had reached a couple of orgasms through my oral stimulation. I went to work on her with my tongue and in no time she was trembling like her knees were about to buckle from under her. She reached out to the desk for support while I had her clit in my mouth licking it slowly like a kitten cleaning herself. She wanted me inside her and I could only honor her request.

Shauna's booty was so beautiful with skin so flawless, it kept the blood rushing down, maintaining my fully and complete erection. I wanted to take her from behind so I could watch the penetration back and forth while spreading her ass cheeks apart. After wrapping a Magnum condom on me, I bent her over on her stomach across the bed and I penetrated her very slowly. She was quietly moaning and begging me to give it all to her and that just made me more eager to tear her up. I started stroking her slowly and then I picked up the pace while I spanked her ass very delicately. Shauna started calling me daddy and she asked me to spank her harder. The harder I spanked her, the harder my strokes became. By the time I increased the speed of my strokes, Shauna was screaming at the top of her lungs that she was cumming. Ignoring her screams, I banged her harder and harder until her legs started shaking and I reached a climax of my own.

I could see the convulsion coming from Shauna's body like an aftershock from an earthquake. She didn't hide the fact that it was a job well done. She told me that we were going to see a lot of each other when we got back to New York and I was more than fine with that. I knew that Shauna was the type of woman who wanted the best that life had to offer and I didn't really have a problem with that because I was on my way to becoming a successful nightclub owner. However, she needed to be patient with me because it would take me a little time to get there.

Sexing Shauna was almost like a fantasy to me. I had never been with a woman who was so fine, sexy, gorgeous and intelligent at the same time. I had been with plenty of women, but none like Shauna. She was sophisticated and I knew that I could succeed with a woman like that by my side. However, I still had a bad habit of my own that I didn't know how to conquer. I was a womanizer with an insatiable appetite for women and it had nothing to do with any moral values because I had none. I wanted to have as many women as I could and no woman could satisfy me completely no matter how great she was. After sex with Shauna, we lay on my bed and talked about everything and anything. I fed her a lot of bullshit about me and what I was looking for in a woman. On the surface, Shauna should've been able to satisfy my every need, but my needs were huge. I should've been honest and upfront with her, but my ego wouldn't allow it. I was the type of person who wanted every woman that I bedded to be in love with me. I was selfish and I wanted to be a conqueror.

As I lay in the bed with Shauna, telling her all kinds of bullshit that she wanted to hear just so I could keep her around, I was chuckling inside because I knew none of what I was telling her was true at the time. She could've very well been bullshitting me as well, but my ego made me believe that I had satisfied her so much that she was just as impressed with my bedroom skills and nobody had done her the way I did. I felt like my sex was powerful and since so many women had told me how good of a catch I was, I started to believe that I was the ultimate prize.

Chapter 8
The Not So Juicy Details

I could not wait to hear what Myles had to say about Chenille. I knew that they had gone off somewhere, but I did not know where. While Shauna and I were in the room watching television, Myles and Chenille knocked on the door and jokingly demanded for us to stop what we were doing through the door. I threw on my shorts and I got up to open the door for them. By then, Shauna had also put on her dress and ran to the bathroom to freshen up. The fact that I was shirtless confirmed to Myles that I had gotten some from Shauna. I didn't have to say too much to him. He gave me that nod that I knew meant "you old dog". I tried giving him the look to ask if he got some without actually saying the word, but the half-smile on his face gave me the answer that I needed. Myles didn't get any ass from Chenille.

I did not know why he didn't get any ass from her, but I would have killed for a piece of that ass. Chenille had the type of body that could get a man's blood flowing so quickly by just looking at her; making him hope that he would have enough space in his pants to shelter his manhood. Myles had a lot more manners than I did when it came to the ladies, but he was still a dog just like me. He knew how to parlay a good conversation into a one-night stand, but he also had values that I wish I possessed. While Shauna was in the bathroom, Chenille knocked on the door to see if she could go in to join her. She opened the door to let Chenille in and while they were in there talking, Myles and I took the opportunity to discuss the way I tore up Shauna's ass and his own lack of progress with Chenille down "Panty Lane".

55

Don't you know that Negro was falling for Chenille? He had the nerve to tell me that he was feeling Chenille and that he wanted to take things slowly with her. I was thinking to myself that Myles had to be a fool to think that he was ever going to see Chenille again after we left Miami. Chenille did not look like the type of chick who was looking for a boyfriend. She wore the type of outfits that screamed, "Fuck me!" and this Negro wanted to date her. The women that I met in the past that dressed like Chenille usually ended up naked with me after a half hour or so from the time I met them. I figured that Myles must've found out something that I couldn't see in Chenille. Therefore, I gave him the opportunity to tell me what was so special about her. Not that I thought Shauna was a bad person or anything, but she was high maintenance like a mother and I did not have the kind of money for her upkeep at the time.

Myles told me that Chenille was really a nice person and that she was the type of woman that he always dreamed of being in a monogamous relationship with. No, this Negro was not talking about developing a monogamous relationship with this girl when he was supposed to be getting in her draws. I didn't get it. Myles had never slipped with any girl in the past, why was this one different, I wondered. Myles was a "wham bam thank you ma'am" kind of guy like me in the past. Where was all this crap coming from all of a sudden? Well, it didn't matter much to me because my mission was accomplished and I knew I tore up Shauna's ass and if I never saw her again, that was cool with me.

The four of us hung out together the whole night in our room playing spades. Around two o'clock in the morning, the ladies decided that they wanted to go home. Myles and I walked them back to their hotel and I gave Shauna a long kiss goodnight. Myles only received a little peck on the lips from Chenille. I felt like my boy was slipping. After all the money he spent on dinner, he should've at least copped a feel or a little tongue action. He just got a peck and that was all.

Chapter 9
Caught Off Guard

As Myles and I were walking back to the hotel, he started revealing to me his feelings for Chenille. He felt that she was the perfect woman for him and he didn't want to mess it up by trying to sleep with her on the first date. I had to remind that fool that it wasn't a first date because we had been hanging with these women for a couple of days already. He told me what he really meant was that he didn't want to sleep with her while he was in Miami. Of course, to keep his ego intact, he told me that he could've gotten the draws if he wanted to. I just nodded my head in agreement to satisfy his ego. I knew that there was no way in the world that Myles would've passed up on that ass if he could've gotten it. Maybe I was judging him based on his past actions, but I didn't buy it.

I felt like my ace was slipping on me and we weren't on the same page anymore. For the last few years, Myles and I have always scored with the ladies and it was always easy. I had never heard of any man getting tired of chasing skirts, but Myles was about to prove me completely wrong.

When we got back to New York, I heard the sound of Myles's phone ringing and it was Chenille calling to make sure that he had made it safely back to New York. I was thinking that maybe she wasn't so full of shit after all, but she still seemed like she had game to me. I refused to believe that she was genuine. I told Myles to let me talk to her after he was done. When he handed me the phone I asked her if I could speak with Shauna and she blew up on me. "You can't even say hi or how you doing and you just gonna get on the phone to ask to speak with Shauna?" I didn't even realize that I didn't greet her. I told her I was sorry and I asked her again if I could speak with Shauna. She told me that Shauna was at the counter trying to see if she could upgrade their flight to first class.

She apparently met some football player at the airport who was kicking game to her and he offered to pay to upgrade her ticket to first class so he could get to know her better. Of course, Chenille was taking advantage of the fringe benefits that came along with her friendship with Shauna. After she revealed that little information to me, I didn't even want to speak to Shauna anymore. I said goodbye to Chenille and hung up the phone. On the cab ride back to our house, I was trying my best to convince Myles that the women were nothing but hos who were trying to get what they could out of men wherever they went. Myles didn't agree with me and he was convinced that Chenille was nothing like Shauna. That sucker was falling right into her trap with that little phone call. She knew exactly what she was doing and he got caught off-guard with his feelings.

By the time the taxi dropped me off to my house, Myles and I were in an intense argument about how the two women were hos and how we should have treated them as such. That was my view, anyway. Myles defended Chenille like he was defending the United States against Iraq. I just told him "whatever, man" as I exited the cab. I gave him my half of the cab fare as the driver proceeded to take him home.

59

Chapter 10
Becoming Roomies

When I reached home that day I wondered if I was about to make a mistake sharing an apartment with Myles. We had both wanted to move out of our parents' houses after we graduated from college, but the rent in New York City was so high and there was no way we were gonna be able to afford our own individual apartments. With that knowledge, we decided that a two-bedroom apartment would be our best bet. We had found an apartment in Jamaica, Queens in the Rochdale Community. It was more like a co-op that I decided to buy with a five-thousand-dollar-initial deposit that I had to borrow from my parents. The rent was only going to be $600 a month for a two-bedroom apartment and Myles was more than excited about paying only $300 a month to have his own place. And that included all of our utilities. The fact that many beautiful women also surrounded us in our complex also raised our interest in the place. It wasn't unusual to bump into a couple of professional sisters while walking the hallways of the building.

Myles and I moved into our apartment a week after we started working. We were both excited about our new jobs and the prospect of becoming independent, established and responsible young men. But me, I was more excited about all the women that I had planned on sleeping with and the freedom of bringing them over to my place whenever I wanted to. We lived on the fifth floor of our building and our apartment was to the right of the elevator in the corner with a view of Guy Brewer Boulevard. The view wasn't much, but it was something to look at when we were bored. Occasionally, I would catch a girl with a fat ass coming out of one of those convenient stores on the boulevard and I would call Myles over to watch her with me. Some of the sisters in Queens had ass that was indescribable to me sometimes.

Myles and I didn't have too much money for furniture, so we relied on the generosity of our parents to furnish our place. Myles's parents had an old leather couch in their basement that they didn't have much use for, so they told him he could have it. It was a light brown colored couch, with a sofa bed that they had bought from Jennifer Convertibles. My parents gave me an old leather recliner that my father used to use to watch football when I was a kid. The chair happened to be the same color as the couch. So, we had a complete living room set. There were no tears on the furniture, but they looked old as hell. There were lines running up and down the seat cushion on the chair like it had taken the shape of my father's ass. The only way to compliment the chairs was for us to get an antique coffee table to give the living room that rustic feel. We managed to make our apartment look very decent.

The excitement that I anticipated prior to moving into the apartment was not all. I was working at one of the hottest nightclubs in the city as an assistant manager and I had more clout than most people my age. I figured that my homie and best friend would try to take advantage of that, right? Hell no! He was all wrapped up in Chenille. She was over the house from the minute Myles got home from work until he went to sleep. She even spent the night sometimes. She had completely taken my boy away from me. I was left hanging by my lonesome.

I was still messing around with Shauna, but it was more about her booty and beauty than anything. Shauna had earned the nickname "Big Time" from me because she thought she was big time all the time. Everything out of this chick's mouth was expensive. We couldn't even go hang out in Manhattan without me coming out of my pocket at least a $150. Her booty was starting to get a little costly and I decided to shut the door on her. I wasn't gonna allow myself to get macked by a chick just because she was gorgeous. Also, Shauna was always looking for VIP treatment everywhere she went. She would come to the club and walk right up to the front of the line because she did not believe that people as beautiful as her should wait in line like regular folks. Even the bouncers at the club were getting tired of her attitude. She would ask them to call me every time she came to the club because she did not want to stay in line. It got to the point where I just told the bouncers to keep her ass standing in the front for as long as they could until I was not as busy to see her into the club.

That chick was on some high horse shit. Sometimes, she would stand next to the bouncers for almost an hour waiting for me to come to the door to get her in. She never once realized that, she would have gotten in the club sooner if she had just gotten in line. We even played jokes on her when the weather was cold. We would have her standing outside for long periods of time until her nose started running. What used to get on my nerves was the fact that she thought she was entitled to everything at the club free of charge because she gave me ass occasionally. When I couldn't provide drinks for her on the house, she would find a football/basketball player or somebody else in the VIP section who could afford her. Even when she was inside the club, she made a big deal about being in the VIP section. There was no end to her nagging. According to her, she was the most independent chick in the world.

Chapter 11
A One Man Show

Of course, working at one of the hottest nightclubs in New York City had its perks. The days of allowing Shauna to prance around like she was my girlfriend were over. I realized that she was a user and abuser, so I decided to cut her off completely. We couldn't even maintain a decent friendship. She always tried to somehow use her beauty to manipulate me into thinking that she was the victim no matter what it was that we were discussing. I remember one time she broke down and told me that most men that she met thought she was an airhead because she was so beautiful and she always had to prove to them that there was more beneath the surface. At the same time, she would turn around and brag about the men who took her shopping down on Fifth Avenue to some of the most expensive and exotic boutiques. There were just too many conflicts with her. New York's most wanted did not want to be stressed by beauty. I stepped.

Honestly, it was very hard for me to walk away from Shauna's fine ass. She had it all except for the right attitude. If her attitude were only bearable, I probably would have continued to see her. On beauty alone, she was a perfect ten. But beauty is not everything. After I made the difficult decision to stop sleeping with Shauna for good, I started bringing home some of the fruits of my labor. I am talking about dimes who were willing to give up the panties for VIP access to the nightclub. Not only were these women fine, some of them were as down to earth as could be. In a way, they were helping with my business as well. Sometimes I would have as many as ten gorgeous females and their friends at the club all paying no admission going around dancing and teasing men all night. And what I liked about these fine women was that they ran in a pack like wolves.

I tried to capitalize on the fact that I knew enough fine women to make the club work. Most men who came to that club left with big smiles on their faces. It was the place to be. Many times men are satisfied with just watching beautiful women come and go. It's not all the time that we need to try to sleep with every woman we meet. Of course, I am not talking about myself. I was 24 and horny twenty-three and half hours everyday of the week. I wanted to sleep with every beautiful woman who came my way.

The first few weeks were somewhat lonely to me because I did not have my partner in crime to do my dirt with me. Since Myles started seeing Chenille exclusively, he spent most of his time with her. I could not even get him to hang with me one night out of the week. And when he did come down to the club, Chenille was always on his arm. To avoid total boredom, I started bringing home a different girl every single night. My work hours were a distraction to Myles because he worked a nine to five. Sometimes I brought home screamers who couldn't keep their voices down and I knew that annoyed the hell out of Myles. I tried as much as I could to keep them from screaming, but what could I do when a woman was screaming out in pleasure. Myles had been there before and he should've known that there are more screamers out there than silent women. Who wants to be with a silent woman anyway?

My charades weren't just getting on Myles's nerves; I was also getting on Chenille's nerves. The three nights that she spent with Myles at the house during the week were enough for her to label me a ho. I was a proud ho. I boasted about the number of fine women that I brought to the house. Sometimes Chenille would try to find flaws with some of the women that I brought home and would tell me that Shauna was the best thing that could've ever happened to me. I only wished she were the one sleeping with Shauna. She would have had a totally different perspective.

I can admit that there were times I brought home women that I thought were beautiful the night before and they turned out to be not so hot the morning after, but that was rare. I always tried to leave room for error. In addition, I would say that mine was plus or minus seven percent. I do not know if sometimes quantity mattered more to me instead of quality, but I banged more girls during my fist two years working at the club than I ever did my whole entire life. I tried as much as I could to be discreet with the women that I was sleeping with, but occasionally, I would have a distressed customer following me around making sure that I didn't leave the club with anyone other than her. I even got the bouncers involved in my charades. Sometimes they were my lookouts and I had to reward them by allowing them more than one guest at the club on special event nights.

Chapter 12
Missing My Homie

While I thought I was having so much fun sleeping with these women, something was still missing in my life. I was missing my best friend. Myles and I grew further apart as his relationship with Chenille became stronger. Even something as spontaneous as a pick-up game of basketball had to be planned. Chenille was always around, keeping a tight leash on Myles. To make matters worst, I found out that she thought I was trying to corrupt Myles by bringing so many different women over to the house. This chick was judging me because I was doing things in my own home. She was lucky that I treasured my friendship with Myles; otherwise she would have been banned from the house.

Back in the day, Myles and I used to kick it hard, especially with the women. We slept with so many women back in college I never thought that he would get trapped like that. That boy was pussy whipped and he couldn't remove the spell from which he was under. I remember one particular time when Myles and I went away to Atlanta for Freak Nik. We met these two young ladies at club One Twelve the very first night we went out. They were visiting from Tennessee and when we told them that we were from New York, they were all over us. We spent half the night dancing with the ladies and by the time we were ready to leave, Myles had convinced the two women that we were dancing with and a third friend to come to our hotel for a nightcap.

Myles had game. When we brought these women to our room, we had brew waiting for them. Everybody was

67

getting nice from drinking rum and coke and before we knew it, we were playing strip spades. I know that most people play strip poker, but the ladies didn't know how to play poker so we made up our own rules for strip spades. Before the night was over, we had all three women butt naked in our room and a free for all orgy ensued. Myles had one girl screaming at the top of her lungs as he banged away at her pussy, forcing her to plead with him to stop because he was too much for her. It was something like a porno flick when the girls decided that it was okay for us to use our video cameras to record them. Myles was trying his best to do his Mr. Marcus impression while I turned my girl into Tracy Lords and did things to her that only Long John Silver would do.

These three freaks were sucking on each other, sucking us, and doing tricks with their pussies that we had never seen before and Myles was right in the thick of it with the camera. While I sat on the bed getting a blowjob from one of the girls, Myles penetrated her from behind and asked one of the other girls to videotape the whole thing. One of the other girls decided to sit on my face while I received head from her friend and Myles banging away at her pussy. It was like a train and we captured the whole thing on camera. That's one of the reasons why I can't understand how Myles got caught up with Chenille.

I still have a copy of that tape in my room and every time I watch it, I keep wondering what happened to him. I am not trying to take anything away from Chenille, but I have brought some banging ass chicks home with me that Myles could have gotten with, but he was never interested. Chenille is fine, but not fine enough to have

Myles under her spell. I'm not *really* trying to relive past experiences, but it does get lonely sometimes *even* when I have a couple of chicks in my room having a threesome. These are experiences that should be shared with my boy, but I didn't have my best friend anymore.

I could only reminisce about the old days when Myles and I used to have as much fun as we wanted chasing women all over New York and down south. We did not miss a Howard University homecoming; we never missed Hampton University's homecoming; we even went as far as Atlanta to Clark University's homecoming; and we always scored with the ladies. Sometimes, we would wait until the last minute to book our hotel when we attended some of these events. Most of the time, we ended up sleeping in some girls' rooms that we met and that was the exciting part of the whole experience. The Bayou Classic in New York was a tradition for me and Myles until Chenille came along. All of a sudden, she is interested in football and she has to attend the game with us. It just was not the same watching that game with Chenille and her partner in crime Shauna.

Chenille claimed she loved football, but she kept asking Myles what did this and that mean after every play. Her fronting ass did not want me to spend any time alone with my boy. Even Shauna was trying her best to kick game to me. I was through with that ass and I didn't want anymore of it.

Chapter 13
From the Projects to the Club

During the period of the last couple of years, Shauna had gone back to school to get her MBA. I was actually happy that she was able to go to school and earn a master's degree in business administration. In fact, I was impressed. I even offered the club to her so she could have a graduation party. Since Shauna did not have too many female friends, she simply asked me to make the VIP section of the club available to a few members of her family, which I did.

I had no idea that she had an uncle Fester. This cat came in wearing a suit that was probably recalled for catching fire because the fabric was so hard. It was 1996 and this dude showed up wearing a checkered suit, white belt and white shoes. Her family had projects written all over them. In addition, I could tell that they hadn't been out in over a decade. With the exception of her mother, the rest of the family hadn't seen fashion since Good Times went off the air. As a birthday present, I also offered Shauna free drinks for her guests all night. That was the biggest mistake that I could have ever made. Now, I had created an atmosphere with a bunch of intoxicated project folks who didn't know how to act in public. They were using words like "You dig" like it was the seventies. Some of them even tried to threaten my regular customers. The men acted like the fact that they were in VIP was an all access pass for them to go around the club to harass the women.

Uncle Fester had more than a few complaints about him. He kept pinching the waitress' ass every time she brought a drink over and he thought fifty cents was a big tip for a drink. This dude actually asked for change back after he gave the waitress a dollar and he wanted to cop a feel for his fifty cents. I had to use one of my bouncers to monitor her family the whole night. The funny thing about men who grew up in the seventies was that they thought they could put a whipping on anybody. They forgot about a new toy call the handgun that most people use today to settle their differences. Uncle Fester and his nephews started messing with the wrong girl and her drug dealing boyfriend, Dave, was a big spender who was known to walk around with a crew that was twenty deep and strapped. I could tell where this thing was about to escalate to after old Fester tried to grab the girl's ass on the floor.

It was time to shut down Shauna's graduation party. Uncle Fester and all the rest of her relatives had to go. These people were like a clan of country folks who hadn't changed their ways from the time they moved from South Carolina in the seventies to the projects in New York. I knew that my bouncers didn't want to be caught in the middle of a fight between a gang of drug dealers and a group of southern folks who still thought that people settled their differences with their knuckles.

I told Shauna that her family had to go because of the liability and threat they posed to the club. When she told them that I was shutting down the party, these people were pissed at me. I was trying my best to keep drug dealing Dave from trying to prove to his hood rat girlfriend that nobody messed with him. He was not the most intelligent person, so I used reversed psychology on his dumb ass. I simply made him feel like he was a made man and made men didn't handle their business in public. That fool bought all the crap that I dished out to him. I didn't care whether or not he settled his beef with Shauna's family; I just did not want it to happen anywhere near my club. The last thing I needed at the club was a shoot out. I didn't want the city to shut us down because of something that had nothing to do with the club.

I admit that Dave wasn't the nicest guy, but he spent a lot of money at the club. Everyone knew he was a drug dealer, but what difference did it make to me? As long as he wasn't selling drugs inside the club, I didn't give a damn. I knew for sure there were a bunch of women who came to the club looking for guys like Dave. Some of these chickenheads used to come to the club looking for drug dealers to buy their drinks and everything else. I made sure that my bouncers kept their eyes on every known drug dealer who walked through the doors.

After we cleared out Shauna's clan, Dave was trying to ask me where they were from. I told him from the way they looked, they had to be from down south somewhere and his dumb ass bought it. Dave was from the Bronx and Shauna's family lived on the east side, downtown in the Chelsea projects. The chances of them ever crossing paths again were slim to none. I was just happy to get the situation under control before it got out of hand. As bougie as Shauna was trying to act all the time, she was just a project girl from a country ass family. I understood then why she wanted to distance herself from everything that was ghetto and low class. She had been receiving an overdose of it at home. Shauna's mother was the only person who showed any type of class.

Chapter 14
New York's Most Wanted

Getting Shauna out of my hair once again was going to be a struggle. The night after the party, I couldn't help myself. As country as I thought Shauna's family was, she was still a standout and she looked as gorgeous as ever the night of the party. She called me when I was leaving the club and wanted me to pick her up from her house to come home with me. I had a couple of chicks with me that I had banged in the past, but they couldn't compare to Shauna. I think Shauna purposely wore her cat suit to the club that night to show off her assets. I was trying my best to avoid looking at her, but this girl was addictive and poisonous at the same time. My wallet wasn't big enough for her, but my dick kept asking me "what difference does it make?" You know whenever a man is thinking with two heads, the southern head always gets the upper hand. I gave in to the booty. Shauna's flawless skin and beautiful smile always got to me.

I picked up Shauna that night and I took her home with me. We had incredible sex for a good two hours before we went to sleep. Shauna did things to me that night that she had never done in the past. I didn't know if it was her way of apologizing for her family's rude behavior at the club, but I accepted her apology. She started in the car when I picked her up. She reached over to my crotch and unzipped my pants to pull out the snake. Before I knew it, she was laying across the console in my Honda Accord and she was blessing me with the best oral stimulation that I had ever received from her. Shauna was working my snake like it was her pet. I was shaking as I bobbed and weaved out of traffic. There was a guy driving a semi trailer alongside of me who clearly saw Shauna pleasing me because he gave me the thumbs up, but she didn't care. She continued to indulge herself with a mouth full of pleasure.

By the time I arrived to my apartment in Queens, I had climaxed inside Shauna's mouth at least once when I stopped at a red light. She didn't even squirm as she swallowed my semen like Nestle milk. We went inside my apartment and I pinned her against the kitchen table, kissing her and sucking on her breasts, praying and hoping that Myles was fast asleep because I didn't have the patience to wait to get to my room before I started tearing her beautiful ass to pieces. Being impatient forced me to do something that I never did in the past. While going through my pockets searching for a condom as I kissed on Shauna's breasts, she pulled my manhood out and slipped it inside her before I could say wait. I had no idea that her cat suit was down to her knees while I was sucking on those humongous breasts. I was already halfway in and I couldn't stop. I started stroking Shauna as hard as I could and I had to place my hands over her mouth to keep her from screaming.

Not wanting to cause her any pain, I asked Shauna if it felt good to her. She nodded "yes," as I continued to tear her up with force. I picked her up and moved her to the washing machine where she sat back with her legs spread wide open as I slid my dick in and out of her. Shauna never felt so good. I looked like a penguin with my pants down around my ankles as I banged away at Shauna. I pulled myself out of her while she sat on the washing machine because I wanted to taste her. While she supported herself with her head against the wall, I ate

Shauna until she screamed that she couldn't hold it in anymore. She let out a loud scream that she was cumming, almost waking up Myles and Chenille. I figured Myles and Chenille had probably been asleep for a couple of hours because they had stopped by the club briefly to drop off a gift for Shauna.

I carried her over to my bedroom walking like a penguin. When I reached my bedroom, I kicked off my shoes and pulled my pants off and Shauna's cat suit off of her. I took a step back to watch her for a couple of seconds before I penetrated her once again. My dick was doing nothing but sticking up the whole time and Shauna was grinning wide because she knew that I was addicted to her body and beauty. I asked her to lie down on her back on my bed with her legs spread open so I could eat her some more. I got so much pleasure out of eating Shauna because I knew it made her weak. After making sure she came a few more times, I inserted my ten inches inside of her and we humped, rode and made each other cum until six o'clock in the morning.

I could never get enough of that girl. I think I went to sleep while I was still rock hard inside of her. I was just exhausted. I had reopened old wounds when Chenille woke up to find Shauna in my apartment walking around wearing one of my shirts the next day. She could not keep from asking Shauna "Why are you still messing with this dog? Don't you know he's been screwing the whole City of New York?" I told Chenille to mind her own business. She even told Shauna about my threesomes and she had gone too far. My threesomes were private and personal. I yelled for Myles to come get

his woman before I lost one of my feet up her ass.
Chenille and I just couldn't get along.

While I thought I was God's gift to the women of New
York City, Shauna thought she was the perfect physical
specimen God had created for men. I couldn't deny that
she was beautiful, but this chick started tripping after she
got her Master's Degree. All of sudden, regular brothers
weren't good enough for her. She even told me that I was
lucky she was still allowing me to sleep with her. Now,
she was on some professional athlete shit all the time.
Some of the players from the New York Knicks, Jets and
Giants used to come by the club and some of them tried
their hardest to push up on her. Shauna wanted to remove
herself completely from the label groupie, so she made
sure these guys chased after her. However, like any other
project chick who wasn't used to a lot of money, she was
bound to give up the draws after the players took her to a
luxury suite at the Ritz Carlton or to their mansion in the
suburbs. Shauna was giving up the goods and she wasn't
getting nothing but a good meal out of it or an occasional
pair of Gucci shoes.

She swore to me she never slept with any of the athletes
who came to the club, but brothers can't keep their
mouths shut about bedding a beautiful woman. I used to
hear the stories all the time from the players and I always
pretended as if I didn't know Shauna. Shauna had
become New York's most wanted and she was being
passed around like a football, basketball, baseball and
even a hockey puck. She was trying her best to use that
MBA to land a husband in the NBA, NFL or MLB, but
they would all remain acronyms to her.

After Shauna realized that she was being used by these athletes, she tried to work her way back into my heart. I wanted to keep hitting it with no strings attached, and that I did. Shauna became my booty call and I used her as much as I could because I was a little hurt when she started sleeping around.

Chapter 15
Energy Fuel

Knowing that Shauna thought she was better than me because she had gotten her master's degree and had also gotten a job earning close to a six figure salary just fueled me with energy and determination. I wanted to show her that those athletes were no better than I was and that I could earn just as much money as they did and even more. For two years, I studied the market for nightclubs while I set aside a huge portion of my salary to purchase my own club one day. Meanwhile, I continued to hear Shauna talk bad about the regular brothers that she met, calling them losers because most of them were just earning $40,000 or $50,000. I felt better because I was earning close to $100,000 myself. However, my father was one of those brothers she was dogging, because he was earning about fifty grand. With that fifty-thousand-dollar salary, he was able to provide for his family and made sure that my brother and I received a college education as well as a stable home while we were growing up.

I didn't even think that she realized that I took my anger out on her every time we had sex after one of her conversations where she dogged people. She intensified my energy to tear up her pussy because she made me sick to my stomach. There were times when I fucked her until she started bleeding. She was repulsive to me because she totally removed herself from regular folks after she started earning a lot of money. However, the funny thing about Shauna was that despite her high salary, she was only able to afford a studio apartment in Manhattan. She refused to buy a two-bedroom condominium in Brooklyn

78

at my urging. She wanted to be in Manhattan in a cramped apartment that she was renting for almost $1500 a month. She loved telling people that she lived on the Upper East Side.

Shauna looked down on everyone who lived out of Manhattan, including me. She always apologized when she caught herself dogging people who lived in Brooklyn, the Bronx and Queens. She felt that Manhattan was the center of everything and only the "haves" could live there. Everybody else was less than, according to her. In a way, I was kind of glad that Shauna was in my life because her bougie attitude kept me grounded. Shauna reminded me of people like Madonna who suddenly develop a British accent because they have money, totally forgetting that they came from the ghetto and probably still have family living in the ghetto.

I felt for all the people in the ghetto who never made it out and I wanted to do what I can to represent them in a way. I wanted to prove to the Shaunas of the world that people are people no matter where they are from and not everyone can be fortunate in life. We cannot live in a society where everyone is fortunate because it's by design. The United States government has enough money to wipe out homelessness, hunger and poverty, but they choose to ignore all three because it all comes down to economics. It's survival of the fittest and not everyone is as fit as Shauna, and she needed to recognize that. Not everyone is meant to be great in life and the law of averages proves that in almost every aspect of life. In basketball, we have the great Michael Jordan; in golf, we have the overly confused, but great Tiger Woods; in football, we have the undeniable Mike Vick, Peyton

Manning and the great Jerry Rice; in medicine, we have
the great Dr. Ben Carson; and in literature, we have the
great James Baldwin, Alice Walker, and Stephen King.
Everyone else just falls in between in almost every
profession and some just fall to the bottom all together.

I was finally able to buy my own nightclub after two
years. It wasn't as big as the one where I worked but it
was my own. It had two floors, with the main dance floor
on the first floor and a small lounge on the second floor. I
didn't have too much money for decorations, so I
brought a few of the women that I was sleeping with to
help me make it look presentable. They tried but it
wasn't good enough. I later learned from a beautiful
woman who was an interior designer that people can do a
lot with fabrics. In no time, she had the place looking
fabulous with different curtains on the walls and the right
lighting. She didn't even charge me for the job and I
didn't even have to sleep with her.

Chapter 16
In With the New

I had no idea what her name was, but she was a beautiful dark-skinned sister who had her own designing firm in Brooklyn, run from her house. She was only 25 and I was 27 at the time I met her at the old club where I used to work. She was actually the first dark-skinned sister that I met without a hang up about her complexion. She was very comfortable in her skin and I liked that very much. There was something about her that drove me wild, but it was subtle. She was confident and determined. I could tell that she was very selective when it came to men. I only saw her at the club once before and I was too afraid to approach her. Half the men in the club were admiring her and I did not have enough confidence to say anything to her. She even shut down all the athletes who thought talking to her was automatic because the rest of the world knew them. And that's one of the things I admired about her. She wasn't impressed with athletes, status or money.

It would take a few months before she returned to the club. I knew she wasn't a club head because most people, who came to the club once, returned at least once a month thereafter. The fact that she stayed out of the clubs worked to my benefit because she wouldn't be there when I was flirting with the slew of women that I needed to flirt with on a nightly basis to keep the club operating successfully. I was actually looking forward to seeing her at the club again. Every night when we opened the club I anticipated her beautiful chocolate skin glowing under the neon light at the entrance and a sparkle in her smile as she sees me standing there waiting with my arms open

81

for a warm embrace. It was just my imagination at work, but I knew that she would come back one day.

Finally, after about nine months since her first visit, she decided to pay us a second visit at the club. This time, I was going to be straightforward and direct without holding anything back. I didn't even notice when she made her way towards the bar. She looked as good and bold as ever. She wore her hair natural and very close to her scalp. Most people would refer to her hairstyle as bald, but I preferred to call it sexy. I could tell that she wasn't wearing much make-up as the shiny light at the bar caressed her beautiful natural skin. The sexy lip-gloss she wore was fondling the fullness of her lips as they shined under the light as well. She wore a beautiful close-fitted sheer top, exposing her navel and a pair of tight-fitted jeans and open-toed sandals. She probably fluctuated between the sizes four and six and the dimensions on her body were perfect. She was very curvaceous with a tiny waist and a flat stomach. She was about five feet five inches tall and weighed about one hundred and fifteen pounds. I could feel the wind beneath my wings moving me in her direction as I effortlessly made my way towards the bar to introduce myself.

When I finally reached her, I almost froze because I was taken by her beauty. Her beautiful smile lit up the whole club and I took it as an invitation to speak to her. I introduced myself as Ron and she told me her name was Nia. "Are you having a good time?" I asked. "I'm not sure yet because I just got here. Maybe I'll have a better time after I finish my first drink," she said. "What are you drinking?" I asked. "Amaretto sour," she answered.

"I have never had one of those before. It must be a special drink for a special lady to be drinking it," I said. She smiled and asked if I wanted one. Playing along, I allowed her to buy me a drink. I stood next to Nia with my back towards the bartender facing the dance floor with almost a bird's eye view of the place. I still had a job to do while I tried to make Nia's acquaintance. I could see Nia smiling after I accepted her drink. She had the most beautiful teeth and smile and it all looked natural.

After talking to Nia for about ten minutes, I needed to return to work. I told her that I wanted to see her at the end of the night before she left. I disappeared from her sight but I was watching her the whole night. When I was at the bar, I noticed that Nia had given the bartender her credit card to keep an open tab for her. I went to my office and called the bartender to tell him that her drinks were on the house all night, but to hold on to her credit card. I didn't want her to know who I was until the end of the night. I noticed that Nia didn't dance much that night. It seemed like she was looking for somebody special the whole night. She finally danced with this smooth looking brother who was like a broke down version of Denzel Washington. He was good looking, but he wasn't the real thing and he messed up the whole thing when he tried to cop a feel of her ass on the dance floor. She left his ass standing there looking like the buffoon he was. I never got why men would want to try to feel a woman's ass after meeting her for fifteen minutes.

I always enjoyed watching the club through the window in my office on the second floor. There, I could monitor almost everybody and it gave me a pretty good idea about who needed to be under my watchful eyes. We also had special cameras behind the two-way mirror at the bar. I could tell who was stealing from the bar and could tell which one of the bouncers was charging people to come through the back door. Most of the employees never knew how I was able to catch them. They always believed that people were snitching on them, but they were their own worst enemies.

I sensed that Nia wasn't having a good time because she couldn't find whoever it was that she was looking for. She seemed restless and ready to leave the club. I ran back downstairs to tend to her because I was not going to let her leave without getting her contact information. As I approached Nia, I could see a big Kool-Aid smile on her face as she spotted me. "You look like you're about ready to leave," I said to her. "I've been looking for you all night long to dance with you and you were no where to be found. You're an evasive man," she said. "Well, we can dance now and I would never try to avoid you on purpose," I said. She grabbed my hand and led me to the dance floor. They were playing "Only You" the remix by 112 featuring Mase. Nia turned around and started rubbing her ass all over my crotch. I danced about three songs with her before I told her that I needed to go. We walked off the dance floor and I asked Nia for her number. I programmed her number on my cell phone and I promised to call her very soon.

I went back to my office to call the bartender to ask him to charge a dollar to her credit card. Without even looking at the total, I could tell she signed off on the tab and left the club. She took the receipt and placed it in her pocket. The reason why I asked the bartender to only charge her one dollar was because I wanted to know if she was honest. Most people who can get over on paying the full price on a bill would want to do it, but I was surprised when I noticed Nia walking back to the bar with receipt in hand, ready to tell the bartender that he had made a mistake. She had passed my honesty test and I knew for sure that I was going to try to get to know Nia. I called the bartender to tell her that he couldn't fix it because the tab was already rung and that the manager would take care of it.

Nia, however, insisted on the bartender fixing it because she didn't want him to get in trouble. That's when I decided to step in and tell Nia that I was the manager of the club and that was why she hadn't seen me all night. I told her that I would take care of it and it was purposely done because I wanted to see her come back inside the club so I could take one more look at her. She smiled as I gave her a hug before she left. I wanted it to be a sweet and innocent hug, but holding on to Nia's body caused me to have a physical reaction that almost embarrassed me. I had to step back quickly before exposing the embarrassment in my pants.

I knew that Nia was special and I needed to be careful if I wanted to date her. All the other women that I was dealing with would have to remain at a distance for me to have a chance with Nia. And I needed to start with Shauna. I knew that any woman who saw Shauna would feel threatened by her beauty and the last thing I wanted was for Nia to misconstrue my relationship with Shauna. She was a booty call and a friend and that was all. Over time, Shauna had lost her special qualities because she had become so shallow. Every time I had sex with her, I felt that I was using her body to get back at her, but I needed to stop that.

Chapter 17
Easier Said Than Done

Getting rid of all the women that I had in my life before I met Nia was going to be a challenge, but never in my life had I met someone that I was so excited about. Nia was someone special and I wanted to know what it was that attracted me to her. I waited for this girl to walk through my door for almost a year and I had no idea why...at first. All I knew was that she was beautiful, but I was already accustomed to being with beautiful women. There was something mysterious about this woman that kept my attention. I knew she wasn't going to be another conquest because I only imagined her being in my life long-term. The things that I planned on doing with Nia were nothing like I had done in the past and none of it was sexual. I wanted to go on vacations with her; I wanted to ski with her; and I wanted to be alone in a cabin somewhere far away with her. I wanted to hold her and I wanted to have children with her. Nia was what I envisioned whenever I thought about a wife. I had never thought about *having* a wife prior to meeting her.

First of all, I needed to get all the fantasy crap out of my system. I wanted to have one more threesome for the road and my two lady friends were more than accommodating on the night that I decided to take them back to my house. As usual, they waited for me to close down the club to follow me back to my apartment. It was always fun filled nights with these two friends. The first night I met them I was actually at Club Speed in Manhattan. I was dancing by myself in the reggae room when Stephanie approached me. She had been staring at me most of the night, but I didn't pay her any mind. She stood in front of me and started dancing. Soon, she would get a rise out of me when she started to grind on me seductively and I couldn't keep from getting a hard on. Stephanie must've liked the boner on her back because she backed me up against the wall and started grinding on me harder and harder. She even took my hands and placed them on her ass. I started reaching under her mini skirt to feel her smooth flesh wrapped tight around her round booty. As she stood there, dancing with me, her friend Patricia approached us and she got behind me, creating a Ronald sandwich. I was dancing with two fine looking women and I was the envy of every man in that club.

That night, I damned near penetrated Stephanie on the dance floor. She kept grabbing my dick and playing with it along with Patricia. I really wanted to take them home with me that night, but I had an early appointment the next morning with another girl who wanted to take me to church with her. I ended up passing up on the girl's offer to go to church the next day. She was angry with me, but who cares? Later that Sunday, I called Stephanie and we made plans to go to this festival that was going on at Prospect Park in Brooklyn. I met her at the train station on Franklin Avenue in Brooklyn. I had promised to drive her home if she met me halfway. Stephanie was coming from the Bronx and I didn't want to make two trips there.

Stephanie and I walked down to Prospect Park after I parked my car somewhere on Eastern Parkway. It was some kind of Panamanian festival. There was a lot of food and reggae music being blasted from a multitude of speakers. Stephanie and I decided to walk down to a little secluded area away from the crowd and it was there that I started kissing, caressing and fondling every part of her body. Before I knew it, I was ten inches deep inside Stephanie while she was pinned against a tree. I don't know why she kept wearing those mini skirts as nice her ass and legs looked, there was no way that I could help myself. I penetrated Stephanie without wrapping my dick in a condom, but neither of us wanted to stop. I had her wrap her arms and legs around the tree as I stroked her from behind with force and determination. I could hear Stephanie's whispers, asking me to tear her pussy up. The more she asked the more enjoyment I got out of humping her. By the time I pulled my dick out to plaster my semen all over her back, I could see a few people staring at us from afar. Stephanie used her underwear to wipe my juice off her body.

I brought her to my house to continue where we left off at the park. Myles was away with Chenille for the weekend and I had the house all to myself. After walking through the doors, I sat Stephanie on the couch and I proceeded to give her the oral treatment that only a princess deserved. I ate Stephanie until my tongue got tired and while I was eating her, she picked up my phone to call her friend Patricia to tell her how great I was with my tongue and told Patricia that she had to have piece of me. To my surprise, Patricia asked to speak with me and we arranged a date for the three of us to hook up the next day.

To make sure that Stephanie didn't renege on her offer to bring Patricia in for a threesome, I tore her ass up that day, leaving her completely exhausted and out of breath. She was so weak she decided to spend the night at my house. The next day I took her out to breakfast and then we went to her house in the Bronx for her to change her clothes. She had showered with me at my house; all she needed was to change her clothes. She called Patricia and told her that we were picking her up. I took them back to my house and they cooked the last big piece of salmon that I had left in the fridge. It was fun watching Patricia and Stephanie cook dinner in the buff. I was horny and hungry at the same time. My dick was sticking up while my stomach was growling. I popped open a bottle of wine after dinner and before I knew it, I had Stephanie sitting on my chest while I ate her and Patricia sucking every inch of me.

Stephanie was moaning so loudly while I was eating her that Patricia asked to switch places with her. I started to eat Patricia while Stephanie sucked the skin off me. Patricia's clit was long and she enjoyed when I sucked on her pussy lips. It was easier for me to make Patricia cum, but she wanted to keep cumming until my mouth got tired. I asked the ladies to suck me at the same time while I sat on my bed. Stephanie took turns juggling my nuts in her mouth while Patricia licked the head. I had received enough head. I wanted to be inside Patricia. I asked Stephanie to lie down on the bed while Patricia stood on the edge of the bed with her legs spread wide open while I stroked her from behind. Patricia's pussy was a little tighter than Stephanie's and I could see her grimacing every time I gave her a long stroke. I slowed down my rhythm just enough for her to start shaking and screaming to me that she was cumming. She also ate Stephanie until she reached an orgasm and their orgasms had a domino effect on me. I pulled myself out of Patricia and they both took my dick in their mouths as they helped me reach the best orgasm ever.

That's how Stephanie, Patricia and I started having our threesomes. During my last night with the ladies, I made sure it was all worth it as I guzzled down two energy drinks before I left the club. I wore their asses out because they fell asleep very quickly and they were snoring like elephants through the morning. While Patricia was fine with our arrangement, Stephanie was more attached than I wanted her to be. When I told her that it was the last time that I was ever going to be with them, I could tell that Stephanie was angry. The whole time I had been sleeping with these women, I never anticipated that strong feelings would develop between us. Stephanie made it clear to me that she thought we had something more than just sex. She had a point in a way because she and I hung out a lot and I knew that she was not seeing anybody else.

I wanted to tell Stephanie that I started going out with someone new and needed to focus on her, but she made it difficult for me. She started getting all emotional with me, telling me that I turned her out and that she had never done a threesome with anyone before me. It was hard for me to buy it from her because everything seemed so natural between her and Patricia. She did get a little jealous occasionally when we were having our threesomes, but I never thought anything of it. Stephanie also confessed to me that she only agreed to have threesomes with me because she loved me.

Chapter 18
Uncertainties

Ever since I became sexually active, I hardly used protection when I slept around with women and I was starting to worry. I felt that I had been lucky in the past and I wanted to make sure that everything was fine with me before I got involved with Nia. In the past, I always judged the women that I slept with by the way they looked. If they were suspect, I would wear a condom, but if they seemed wholesome enough, I would always take my chances. It was like crap shooting and I was willing to live dangerously. I found it easier for me to trust the women who were college educated and professional. I always believed that they valued their lives and professions too much to risk sleeping with a bunch of men. In a way, I felt somewhat special because they allowed me to sleep with them without protection. I heard the phrase "you're the only one I ever slept with without a condom" quite often. I never came inside a woman since I've been having sex, and I have never contracted any sexually transmitted diseases…that I knew about anyway.

To me, no symptoms meant that I was fine and the women that I had been with were fine as well. If their coochies were odorless, I thought they were safe enough. I had learned that women who had discharges and unfriendly smells were most likely to carry diseases. I always used my finger test to find out if a woman had a fishy smell. If I didn't detect any smell, I thought they were safe. No woman had ever come to me with any complaints about catching something from me either. I just felt invincible when it came to sex and I thought the quality of women that I slept with were immune to sexually transmitted diseases just as I was. I never as much contracted crabs from a woman. Most of my teammates back in college experienced catching crabs or gonorrhea from a woman. I always stayed away from the women who slept with my teammates.

I knew there was only one way to be completely certain that I was disease free, but I was too afraid to find out. I wanted to wait for a sign before I went to the doctor to find out if I was sick. The fear of alienation and people labeling me didn't sit well with me. At the same time, I didn't want to expose Nia to any potential diseases that I was carrying. "The Monster," as they called AIDS in the hood, was what I feared the most. The other diseases, I understood that a penicillin shot or antibiotic could take care of them, but AIDS was a terminal disease and I didn't want to live my life knowing that I was going to die.

Since I was getting sex from plenty of women, there was no need for me to rush Nia to have sex with me. I wanted to take my time with her and she was a good girl who didn't want to rush anything either. I continued to sleep with the women that I was sleeping with without protection until I broke up with each one of them. There was close to a dozen women that I had my last hurrah with. I believed that if I caught something from them it was already in me and there was no need to protect myself. I also assumed that these women saw their gynecologists regularly and more often than not, they would find out if they were infected with any diseases. I was counting on them to find out if they had contracted any sexually transmitted diseases and in turn contact me to find out if it was from me. Since I never received a call from anybody, I assumed I was disease free.

My last sexual escapade was with Shauna. She and I went at it like old times and we enjoyed every minute of it. I started to believe that sex was the only thing that I ever had in common with Shauna. She pleased me in every way sexually and the attention she paid to details during sex was comparable to none. This girl was my true sex partner, but I couldn't stand her as a person. When I told Shauna that I couldn't see her anymore after we had sex for the last time, she blew her top. She couldn't believe that I was willing to let her go. Shauna always believed that she was the cream of the crop, but she wasn't creamy enough for me. I needed to let her go so I could concentrate on building a relationship with Nia.

There were many things that worried me; my future with Nia was one of them, my relationship with the women who had been in my life since I started working at the club, the success of my club and my health. My health was my biggest worry because I had taken so many chances with so many women. However, with Nia in my corner, I thought I could conquer it all and be just as successful on my own as I was when I worked to make somebody else rich.

Chapter 19
Getting Started

Words about my new club spread very quickly and I was able to get a few of the patrons from the old place where I worked to follow me to my new spot. I was also getting serious with Nia. She was an integral part of my nightclub. She sent out mass emails to people about my special events as well as hosted parties for me to let people know that Ron's Hot Spot was the place to be. I had also persuaded my father to invest with me. He had worked as head of security and assistant manager of a club himself, so I didn't have to convince him too much about the possibility of a high income. Not only that, the club business is mostly a cash business. Uncle Sam would always get his share, but the plan was to give him as small a percentage of his share as possible.

With my father as general manager, I as president and Nia as director of marketing, success was definitely reachable. Nia was able to dedicate a lot of her time to my nightclub because she had developed a clientele with her own company where she didn't have to work too much to make a lot of money. A couple of gigs a week were enough for Nia to live a luxurious life and most of her clients were people who lived on Fifth Avenue or right in midtown Manhattan. Nia could earn enough money in a week from one of her clients to chill for three months if she really wanted to. She was earning big bucks. I was falling head over heels for Nia and for the first time I could see why Myles was blinded by Chenille. It was the love bug getting to me just like it got to him.

One of the things that I explained to Nia was the fact that I had to be friendly with the women who frequented the club because as far as entertainment goes, wherever the women were, the men would follow. I kept in touch with a few of my ex-booty calls. And some of them were eager to receive a lifetime pass to my club. Certain women had to have VIP status to the club every week because there were so many men after them. All they had to do was tell their courters where they would be, and they would follow like mice chasing cheese. Most men would go to the end of the world to meet women.

It took a little time, but the club started flourishing a few months later. We were at capacity from Wednesday night through Sunday night. We closed on Mondays during the summer and we had special parties on Tuesdays. During the football season, we hosted Monday night football at the club and it was a hit because our scantily clad waitresses were always something to see. The ladies had decided to wear the skimpy outfits to earn their tips from the many men who came to the club to appease them. Overall, the money started rolling in and I decided to pay Nia a handsome salary for helping to make Ron's Hot Spot the hottest club in New York. My dad and I were partners, so we both paid ourselves a good enough salary to maintain our lifestyles. Everything else was invested in the club or remained in the business account.

Nia never displayed any sign of jealousy while we worked side by side. She understood that I had a job to do in order to obtain any kind of success. She was confident that our relationship was solid enough to weather any storm or anything that was thrown our way. I admired the fact that she had enough confidence in me to allow me to go out to the club almost every night of the week to do my job without hassling me. I also hired a street team and I made sure they blasted the whole city of New York with posters and fliers about the club for six months straight. And I wasn't shy about throwing on my jumpsuit and sneakers to hit the street with a bunch of guys, who worked for VIP access to the club, in order to make the club a success.

My street team was comprised of mostly college-aged kids who wanted to hang out at the club. Most of them never had to pay for drinks and they were allowed to bring their friends to the club free of charge. I allowed that to happen for almost six months until the club started picking up. Then I had to sit them down and explain to them that running the club was a business and I could not allow them to keep bringing their friends to the club without paying admission anymore. I proposed a new deal to them. I told them that I would give them $100 for every ten paid customers they brought to the club. They had to make sure that their customers' names were checked off at the front desk so they could be paid at the end of the night. It was also a way for them to earn money while they partied. They still drank on the house, but their friends had to pay.

The flip side of the deal that I had with them was that if they failed to bring ten people, they would not be compensated at all. I had about twenty kids working hard to bring ten people each to the club five nights a week. The cover charge was $20 on most nights, so you do the math. The marketing plan that I used for the club has been a total success and a couple of those kids now work for the club on a full-time basis. We've even expanded the club a little to accommodate our growing clientele. We have had some of the best security personnel since our opening. Security was one of our top priorities. Whenever someone threw a punch inside the club, it took half a second for security to throw their ass out on the pavement. And if they even thought about retaliating, the detail officer standing in front of the club was more than willing to bust a few caps to keep a few Negroes in check.

No stone was left unturned. My dad and I planned strategically to have a bird's eye view of the place at all times. One of us was always on the second floor monitoring the action in the club; we had bouncers on every corner of the club; and a couple of floaters to make sure things went accordingly. The radios the bouncers carried were top of the line because I never wanted any confusion. My father personally trained every bouncer who worked for us. Having a second-degree black belt in karate, my father was able to teach the guys techniques to take people down very quickly.

Chapter 20
Getting Engaged

After dating for almost three years, Myles and Chenille decided to get engaged. Myles wanted my blessing before he asked Chenille to marry him. Even though we were roommates, Myles and I had not been spending too much time together. I was very busy trying to get the club off the ground and he was busy working all kinds of overtime to save enough money to buy Chenille a big two-carat rock. Myles was also the type of person who wanted to do things right. He did not just want to marry Chenille, he wanted the house, the picket fence and everything else he felt associated with a happy marriage.

Myles worked very hard to save enough money to buy a ring, help pay for his wedding and a down payment on a house. The money for the wedding was not really necessary because Chenille's parents were loaded and as spoiled as she was, I knew that Myles could not afford to pay for the kind of wedding she wanted. Clearly, her parents were going to have to pay for her wedding. Myles still wanted to play his role as a man in case he had to help contribute to the wedding.

I really did not know why I couldn't stand Chenille, but I knew she was the right woman for Myles. Sure, they had their little disagreements, but they never lasted too long. Chenille knew how to pamper Myles and she motivated him to become one of the top engineers at his firm. Myles was also good for her because he had a passive personality. He was always supportive of her and he made sure he encouraged her to pursue anything she wanted. When Chenille decided to leave the firm of

99

Arthur Anderson after successfully taking the CPA exam, it was Myles who encouraged her to start her own accounting firm.

As bad as I made her sound, I really had nothing but love for Chenille. She was the one who looked out for me every year when Uncle Sam was trying to reach too deep in my pockets. Chenille and I may not have gotten along well, but I recognized that she was a good accountant. Business was business regardless of our friendship. She minimized my taxes as much as she could every year and if Uncle Sam had ever decided to audit my company, I knew I was in good hands. She and Shauna were starting to grow apart as friends as well. Shauna was all about the spotlight while Chenille wanted to live a quiet family life with Myles. Chenille didn't make a big deal of the next big entertainment event happening in New York City. She could care less about VIP and red carpet treatment. Her focus was her relationship with Myles and establishing her business.

Overall, I thought Chenille was a pretty decent person for Myles and I knew that she would be a good wife for him. She always made sure that no one took advantage of Myles's kindness. She was the domineering personality in the relationship, but she allowed Myles to be the man when he needed to be. It was an arrangement that worked for them. I couldn't see myself dating a woman who thought she had to allow me to be the man when I needed to be. Since Myles was fine with it, there was nothing I could say about it.

I offered to host Myles's engagement party at the club in the lounge on the second floor. It was a private event

separate from the club and only Myles's friends and
family were invited. A few of Chenille's folks were there
as well, but only the ones that Myles knew about. Myles
had planned a spectacular party and everything went
accordingly. He took Chenille out to eat earlier during
the day on a Friday and after they were finished with
dinner, he told her he wanted to come by my new spot to
check it out. At first, she didn't really want to see my
face, but she gave in to him after he told her he wanted to
dance the night away with her.

Chenille was also a softie in her own right. Myles got to
the club around midnight and one of the bouncers gave
me the signal when he arrived at the club. The DJ asked
everyone to clear the dance floor and the spotlight was
brought down on Myles in the middle of the dance floor.
He knelt down on one knee and extended his hand out to
Chenille, "I have been having the best time of my life for
the past couple of years and I can only see better times
ahead and I don't want to stop the ride. You brought
changes to my life that made me a better man and there's
no other person I would love to spend the rest of my life
with than you. Chenille, will you marry me?" he pulled
the two-carat diamond ring out of his pocket. Chenille
was elated because she had no idea. All of her friends
and family were upstairs looking down at her. She said
"yes," emphatically.

Myles brought down the house with his proposal. I think
every woman in the club that night wanted to marry
Myles. The DJ announced that the engagement party
would continue in the second floor lounge where
Chenille's and Myles's family and friends were waiting.
Even Nia got teary eyed at Myles's gesture. Champagne

was on the house as we celebrated my man's engagement. We had food, cake and party favors in the lounge for them. I also bought Myles a designer watch by Kenneth Cole as an engagement gift.

The party went well except for the fact that Shauna kept cutting her eyes at Nia like she did something to her. I could tell Shauna was a little jealous of Nia, but Nia never even acknowledged her. I had already told Nia about Shauna ahead of time and she expected Shauna to act like a little brat. I tried my best to be cordial to Shauna, but she insisted on making smart little comments about Nia. She thought Nia's hair was cut short because she couldn't grow any. She was shocked when I pulled out a picture of Nia out of my wallet wearing hair longer than hers. Nia had decided to cut all her hair off because she was tired of wearing a perm. My woman was confident and she was affectionate the whole night. Even the bench-warming player from the Knicks that Shauna was sporting noticed her dirty looks towards Nia. He slipped out the door without saying a word to her. He figured she was a little too envious of Nia and that meant that she was not over me yet.

Chapter 21
Finally

Nia and I had been dating for a few months and I couldn't stand the celibacy anymore. I could tell that Nia was also getting hot for me as well. She and I hadn't been out or done anything since I bought the club. We really had no personal or leisure time to hang out. Like I said, Nia was very understanding, so she didn't press the issue. She understood that I was trying to get my business off the ground and spending time with me was the least of her worries. We did, however, eat lunch together almost every day. I used to bring special picnic baskets to her home office. Nia worked from her loft apartment in Brooklyn because it was more convenient for her. I loved her place because it was artsy and eclectic. She was definitely a whiz in the world of interior design.

On a Monday night when the club was closed, I decided to take her out for a special dinner. We were in the mood for Thai food, so we decided to go this little Thai restaurant on Seventh Avenue in Manhattan. It was one of my favorite Thai restaurants and I wanted to take the opportunity to show off my culinary knowledge to Nia. Unbeknownst to me was the fact that it was also Nia's favorite restaurant. The waiters there knew us both by name. We found it funny that we both liked the same restaurant in all of New York City.

We sat at the restaurant for close to two hours having dinner and conversing about life in general. I enjoyed listening to Nia talk and I never got tired of hearing her tell me about her dreams to one day become "the most sought-after" interior designer in the country. Her dreams were bigger than New York. Nia's plan was national and I admired her courage and determination to make it all happen. After dinner, we took the train down to Central Park and there we took a horse and carriage ride. I held Nia in my arms and this feeling to be with her all the time took over me. Nia and I had never discussed our relationship and I didn't know where she stood as far as our progress. I wanted to make sure that she knew that I didn't want to share her with anybody else. I felt like a little boy back in high school as I asked Nia to be my girlfriend. "I thought I was already your girlfriend. You think I would spend my valuable time with just anybody." she replied with a kiss. "I just wanted to make sure that you knew that it was official," I said to her as I kissed her back. "Nowadays everything has to be spoken so there are no misunderstandings," I said with a smile on my face. "You're trying to sound all old-school. What do you know about the old days?" she said, laughing at me. "Well, when I was a young man chivalry was a big thing," I said jokingly. Nia and I laughed at the conversation while we held on to each other.

We left Manhattan that night around eleven o'clock and went straight to Nia's apartment because I had left my car parked in front of her house. That night was the first time Nia had ever invited me to spend the night with her. I never waited so long to sleep with a woman and it was somewhat refreshing to me. After almost nine months, she was ready to let me make love to her and it was love because I knew that I had fallen for Nia. In the past, I had sex with many different women, but I never made love to any of them. I cannot honestly say that I had gone without having sex for nine months, because I slept

around for the first five months of our relationship. I did
not consider it cheating because I never thought we were
an item until this special night. My conscience was clear,
and it was my way of consoling myself. At least it made
me feel better knowing that I did not consider us dating
exclusively for the first five months. Whether or not Nia
went out with other men during that time, I didn't care to
know. I only cared that she officially became my woman
that night.

Anyway, when I got upstairs to Nia's place she asked me
to have a seat in her living room. As I sat there watching
television, Nia went upstairs to run a warm bath in her
tub. I knew that's what she was doing because I could
hear the water running. I thought she was trying to get
cleaned up before she gave me some. I was surprised
when she came back downstairs wearing a silk robe and
asked me to follow her upstairs. When I got to her
bathroom, which was connected to the master bedroom, I
found that she had set the mood with candles and a warm
raspberry scented bubble bath. She disrobed and asked
me to get in the extra large tub to join her. It must have
taken me less than ten seconds to take all my clothes off.
I couldn't wait to hold Nia in my arms while we sat in
the tub. I also noticed a chilled bottle of chardonnay in
the corner with two glasses.

After I got undressed, I stepped in the tub with my back
against the back wall with Nia sitting between my legs.
She asked me to pour us a glass of chardonnay and I
obliged. It was soothing to just chill in the jetted tub with
Nia. I was holding on to my woman and I was proud. I
have to admit that I was rock hard as I wrapped my
hands around Nia to hold her, and I am sure she could

feel my manhood all over her back like an attacking snake. Nia was very independent and she melted my heart in every way. We sat in the tub until the water got cold and all we talked about was our upbringing. I learned that Nia grew up with her mother in the Canarsie section of Brooklyn. Her mother was a bank executive who raised her alone. Her father walked out on them when she was ten years old. He left her mother for a younger woman. Other than the child support check that her mother received from him every month, they never had any contact with him. She never even tried to find him. She was hurt that he walked out on her without ever coming back, at first, then she slowly moved on. She said when he was around he was a very good husband and father. However, after he met his mistress he became a new man and he changed for the worst.

Nia's mom never remarried, but she had been dating her boyfriend for almost fifteen years. Her mom's boyfriend was a very nice man who treated her like his own daughter. She called him her adoptive dad. Nia was at peace with herself because she had proven to her father that he made a mistake when he turned his back on her. Her mother was especially proud of her independence. After Nia graduated from college, she worked as an apprentice under this woman who was a well-known interior designer in New York. It was there that she honed her skills as a designer and she was able to start her own company and establish her own clientele.

One of the most important questions I had for Nia was why she was single when I met her. "I had been dating this jerk who cheated on me with another woman, and I only found out he was cheating because the other woman had gotten pregnant. She somehow was able to find my number and called me to tell me about her pregnancy," she said. "When I confronted my boyfriend, he denied the whole thing. However, when his new chick decided to set him up on a three-way call, I was down. I heard everything that had been going on between them and I decided to leave the whole situation alone. I dated the jerk for almost five years," she said angrily. "We don't have to talk about this because I can see it was a painful experience for you," I said.

I also assessed the situation for my own good. I didn't know if Nia was the kind of woman who held grudges against all men because one had hurt her, so I was overly careful with her. I had never found Nia to be jealous or feel threatened by anyone and I would have never known that she was hurt in her past relationship until she told me. She did not carry old baggage with her, but I was still careful. It is not all the time that people display their emotions about certain experiences in their lives, and I treasured Nia too much to hurt her.

After we got out of the tub, Nia went to her bedroom and lay down on her back on the bed. She asked me if I could rub lotion all over her body and I was more than pleased. This was the first time that I had ever gotten this intimate with Nia and I did not know whether I should have led or followed. I was ready to go wherever she wanted me to go. While I was rubbing lotion on her back, I decided to give her a massage. I spread my legs across her back with my Johnson erected to its full length to kneel over her like I was sitting on her to give her a massage only befitted for a queen. As I went up and down Nia's back with the lotion, the smoothness of her skin was

107

exhilarating and I wanted to kiss her back. I rubbed my way sensually from her shoulders down to her lower back and when I got near her ass, I decided to make my way back up her back as I could see her pinkness staring me in the eyes. "Why didn't you continue down my ass?" she asked "I'm afraid of what I might do if I get my hands on your ass," I answered. "So, you're gonna let a sister walk around with an ashy ass?" she said jokingly. "No ma'am. I will lotion that booty to your liking as soon as possible," I shot back at her with a smirk on my face.

All I could think about was placing my mouth on her to eat her like a sweet slice of watermelon. I continued to rub her body with lotion. When I got to her ass and started rubbing and squeezing it, she whispered, "I like that. Do it again". I was thinking along the lines of "Can I penetrate you, please? Baby, baby please?" Nia's body was off da hook and I was happy that I got a chance to finally rub my hands all over it. When I was done with her back, she turned over so I could lotion her front. When she turned around and saw all ten inches of my Johnson standing up ready to attack her, she playfully said, "Someone is turned on I see." "Am I the only one?" I asked. "I guess not, but what are we gonna do about it?" she said. That's when I took the initiative to pull her towards me and started kissing her like it was our first kiss ever.

Nia's kisses were passionate and full of life. I took her full lips inside my mouth and started sucking on them and softly kissing them. I moved my tongue slowly inside her mouth savoring her taste buds like they were my own. Her tongue was soft, tasteless, and clean. Her fresh breath forced me to keep my eyes closed as I continued to African kiss her. There was no way in the world that I was French kissing her. Our kisses were too passionate and our lips were too full to be labeled French. African kisses are sexier than French kisses because African kisses involved a lot more tongue and lip tugging. You got to have full lips in order for people to tug on them and I've only seen a limited amount of white people with full lips. Maybe Angelina Jolie might be able to African kiss Mick Jagger one day on the big screen, but for now African kissing is only a black thing. They can keep that French kiss.

As I was kissing Nia, it seemed like the temperature in the room was rising. I went down her neck, to her shoulders with my tongue licking and kissing her body like it was my temple. I arrived at her perky breasts with my tongue landing right on her nipple. I continued to lick and suck until Nia wrapped her hands around my neck, leaned her head back, and said, "Take me! I want you now!" I was more than ready to take her, but first, I wanted to make sure she got a taste of my tongue on her clit and inside her until she couldn't stand it anymore. I slowly stuck my tongue inside of her to taste the sweet juices that I had been yearning for over nine months. She tasted good. I continued to lick her pussy lips while caressing her clit with my fingers. Nia was trying to grab the sheets confirming that she was pleased. I was not done yet. I took her clit in my mouth and slowly dispensed enough saliva on my tongue to moisten her up. Her clit felt so good in my mouth I savored it for close to fifteen minutes while she moaned and groaned. I ate Nia until her body started trembling and she begged me to take her. Before I could take her, I felt the convulsion of her climax while I rolled my tongue around her clit. The fact that she added a little pressure to my head with her inner thighs confirmed that I had taken her to seventh heaven. With her legs tightly wrapped around my head and holding on to the sheets like she needed comfort, I knew she was reaching a climax of high magnitude, so I continued to eat her until the convulsions went away.

Nia wasn't selfish, though. Realizing that I had been pleasing her for the last half hour or so, Nia decided to bring her head down to my crotch while her goods sat on my face in a sixty-nine position. She took me in her mouth and the warmth of her mouth and the movement of her tongue around my dick completely eased my tension and caused me to feel totally relaxed as I continued to kiss and lick her clit until both of us exploded on each other. We weren't done yet. I felt so comfortable with Nia I almost penetrated her raw, but she stopped me in my tracks and asked me to wear a condom. I reached into my wallet and pulled out a Magnum condom. After I unwrapped the condom, Nia took it from me and rolled it down pass the shaft of my penis down to the base ensuring that she was protected and secured.

After making sure everything was well in place, it was time for Nia to take a ride on my horse carriage. She straddled me while I lay down on my back. She slowly eased her way down my ten inches and I could see her grimacing a little, but she wanted it all. After securing a comfortable position with all of me inside of her, Nia proceeded to wind on me and the rhythmic movement of her thighs could only cause a rhythmic reaction of my own. Nia and I fucked each other until she got tired of riding me. She turned around to hold on to the headboard while I penetrated her from behind. Watching Nia's body in motion in front of me was very pleasing and I couldn't contain my explosion anymore. Hearing her pleas for me to slow down because she was about to climax again intensified my own need to climax along with her. After a few good strokes and Nia looking back at me and smiling in pleasure, we both exhausted the last supply of "fluids" left in our bodies.

Nia and I fell asleep on her bed with our bodies wrapped around each other. Making love to Nia was different from any other woman that I slept with in the past. There was something more fulfilling about it. I wanted more of it and maybe even a lifetime of it. I must've fallen asleep with a big smile on my face because I woke up with an even bigger smile on my face the next morning. I found my ten inches inside Nia's mouth under the covers around eight o'clock in the morning and of course, I had to reciprocate. Talk about waking up to a beautiful day? Nia and I went at it for a good hour before we decided to get up and take a shower.

Nia and I did not have enough of each other yet. She ended up canceling her appointments to spend the day with me. After I made her breakfast, she and I got dress and I drove to my house to change my clothes. While we were in Queens, Nia decided to go down to Jamaica Avenue to buy some fabric for a new project she was gonna be working on. Apparently, this man who came by my club was so impressed with her work that he decided to hire her to decorate his club in Long Island. Nia and I spent the whole day doing almost nothing but drive around New York City. Around six o'clock that evening, we went to BBQ's in Manhattan to get a bite to eat then went back to Nia's place to watch television until it was time for me to head to the club, but not before we had another passionate lovemaking session. It was a day well spent and I enjoyed every minute with Nia.

Chapter 22
I've Fallen and I Don't Want to Get Up

The more time I spent with Nia, the more I enjoyed being around her. Sometimes, I couldn't wait to see her. I felt like a little kid who couldn't wait to get to his favorite amusement park. Nia brought joy to every facet of my life and it was definitely something that I wasn't used to. Even my dad started teasing me about getting caught out there. I was known to be the most eligible bachelor who bragged about never settling down to my family. My dad always told me that one day I would think differently, but I didn't expect it to happen at the age of 28.

While I was trying my hardest to suppress my feelings for Nia, she was opening more to me everyday. One night while I was over her house after one of our sexual sessions, Nia told me that she felt complete with me. I wanted so much to tell her that I felt the same way, but something kept me from saying it and I felt badly. I didn't know why I was having such a hard time allowing Nia into my world, but I knew that I deeply cared for her. Honestly, I think I was in love with her. Away from work, I spent all my time with Nia and I even enjoyed watching her work. It was a great situation for us because she worked during the day and I worked at night. Sometimes, I would go to her house while she's working just to watch her work. I reveled in the fact that so many people put their trust in my woman to make their homes and businesses look better. Nia also helped me stay ahead of the competition. Every three months she would change the design inside the club to give it a new look. No one knew what to expect when they came to my club.

I found no flaws whatsoever with Nia. She was my perfect angel and I was happy that she was mine. Holding on to Nia was the most important thing to me. I often saw myself lying across the couch inside a big mansion in Long Island, New York with two kids and a dog and my hot wife, Nia, lying next to me as we watch our children play. It was a fantasy that I wanted to make reality. Nia had my nose open and I really didn't want to close it. For the first time in my life, I was at ease with myself and it was peaceful. I knew that Nia and I were still going through the honeymoon period of our relationship, but I didn't foresee any problems that could separate us.

The feelings that I was experiencing were a little funny to me, so the only person I knew whose nose was more open than mine was Myles. I needed to talk to someone about my feelings for Nia. I knew that I should've been talking to her instead of Myles, but I wanted to make sure that I did things the right way. I had never been in a monogamous relationship, so I didn't know the rules. Women always came and went in my life and none was ever too special. I wanted to find out what was so special about Nia.

Myles and I made plans to go to this local pool hall to kick it. It had been so long since I hung out with my best friend. I was overly excited about seeing him. We lived together, but we hardly saw each other. If Myles was not spending his time at work, he was with Chenille. And the odd hours that I worked didn't help things either. It seemed like my boy had to pencil me into his calendar in order to hang out with me.

I thought it would best if Myles met me at the pool hall. I arrived there before he did and while I was sitting there waiting for Myles, sipping on my beer, this girl who was playing pool at the table a couple of feet from me kept flirting with me. She was a fine looking woman with a great body, but the new Ron was not interested. She kept sticking her ass my way as she seductively caressed the pool stick before every shot. The only thing I could do was chuckle. She was trying really hard, but my mind was somewhere else. I was so lost in thought I didn't even realize when Myles tapped me on my shoulder. "What's up, player? I see that you already have a honey salivating over you," he said. "What are you talking about?" I answered, playing dumb. "You mean to tell me that you can't tell that the woman over at that table is just waiting for you to go up to her and spread her legs open on the pool table to smash the hell out of her?" he said. I laughed and said, "Man, I ain't paying that freak no mind. I have more important things and people to think about. Hey, what are you drinking, Myles?" I said switching the subject. "You know. The usual." he said. I asked the bartender for a Corona.

Myles took his drink and we moved to the empty table across the room. I could tell that the girl was still following me with her eyes and Myles kept teasing me about it. "So, what's up, man? Did you give up booty or something?" he asked jokingly. I quickly changed the subject by asking Myles if he remembered the young lady that I introduced to him the night of his bachelor party and he said "yes." I told him how Nia had been dominating my every thought and she was the only woman that I ever felt that way about, but I was too scared to allow myself to get too emotionally involved.

"What are you afraid of?" he asked. "I'm afraid to be like you, all happy and shit all the time like nothing else in this world matters to you as long as you have Chenille." "And what's wrong with that?" he asked. "People aren't supposed to be that happy all the time. Something is bound to happen to mess it all up and that's when the pain comes out," I said.

"So, you're afraid of pain?" he asked. "No I'm not afraid of pain. I just don't want somebody controlling my emotions," I answered. "What do you mean?" he asked. I was really getting tired of Myles's questions. I was trying to find answers and this Negro kept asking me questions after every statement. "Forget it," I said. "I see. So, you want to forget the fact that you're falling in love with a gorgeous woman who could probably bring you happiness beyond your dreams," he said. Myles was really getting on my nerves. He always had a way of bringing light indirectly to a situation. Myles's approach to solving problems was sometimes nerve wrecking but they were effective. "I got the picture. I see your point. I should just take a chance on love because if I don't do it, I'll never know what could've been," I said. "I didn't say anything. You said it," he followed.

"You might as well take that rack and wear it around your neck like a necklace because I'm gonna whip your ass all night and you're gonna be racking until your hands get tired," I said to Myles. "Here you go talking that shit again. Last time we played, I whipped your ass so bad Harriet Tubman almost woke up from her grave to start a new underground railroad to get your ass out of the pool hall to safety. I was treating you like slave," he said. Myles had his moments with the jokes, but I needed

to avenge the ass whipping that he put on me last time
we played, so I tried to psych him out before I left the
pool hall a victim once again.

Myles and I played "best out of seven" and it came down
to the wire. He was clearing the table when the cue ball
suddenly scratched after he made a double shot. It was
my turn to clear my balls off the table. I made all seven
of my shots, but I missed the last shot for the eight ball. It
was Myles's turn and he had one ball left. He made his
last shot and it was time to shoot the eight ball in the
corner pocket. The cue ball was all the way across the
table and there was no may Myles could clear all that
green to make the shot. I watched and joked around as he
took his last shot. "Unless you're a gardener who's used
to seeing all that green, no way you're gonna make this
shot," I said. Myles laughed and said, "Watch this." He
was able to get the eight ball in the corner pocket, but the
cue ball rolled to the pocket across and just like that he
scratched and I won the game. Of course, we argued that
it wasn't a real win because he scratched, but I didn't
make the rules of the game. As far as I was concerned, a
win is a win.

"So you really care about this woman, huh?" Myles
asked. "Yeah. I like her a lot and I never expected to be
this crazy about any woman. Guys like me don't fall in
love. We hit it and split," I said. "Guess what? You're
growing up, my man. It all has to do with maturity.
That's part of the evolution. You can't continue to do the
same things that you were doing when we were young.
Some of us reach maturity sooner than others, but most
of us reach it at one point in our lives. I just want to be
the first one to congratulate you and tell you to just enjoy

117

the ride because it's a beautiful thing," he said. Myles always had a way with words and I understood exactly what he meant. We gave each other dap then exited the pool hall.

I needed to spend those few hours with my friend because he helped me accept what was happening in my life. Myles has always been frank with me and he always knew the right thing to say when I sought his advice. I figured if I was falling for Nia, I might as well let go because there was no point of fighting it. Nia was everything I wanted in a woman. She was supportive, beautiful, intelligent, affectionate, caring, conscious and most of all, sexy. I used to get an erection just watching her walk. I had to learn to control it through the course of our relationship. Nia stimulated me in more ways than one. However, I enjoyed the intellectual stimulation more in the beginning because that's all I was getting from her. She wanted to make sure that I was going to be around for a long time before she gave up the goods. And I appreciate her for that to this day.

Chapter 23
Here Comes Drama

As time went on, Nia and I became the most beautiful couple in New York City as far as I was concerned. She was my princess and I was her prince. The objective was to always hold her in high regards despite any difficulties we might've encountered. There was nothing about Nia that could ever make me disrespect her. She was too much of a lady for me to muster the courage to disrespect her under any circumstances. Besides, I was falling in love with her and I wanted to do nothing but love her. Nia reminded me of my mother in a way. She was overly caring, but at the same time, she gave me enough space to grow as a man and maybe even a little too much space.

Since Nia spent very little time at the club after it was established, Shauna saw it as an opportunity to get back into my good graces. Like I mentioned before, Shauna's beauty could not be denied, but I had been over her for a long time. I knew that she thought her pussy was good, but it wasn't good enough to keep me around. I was maturing as a man. I needed to come to terms with what I wanted out of life and Nia was it. Shauna was a wannabe baller who was looking for opportunities to floss as much as she could, whenever possible. She hadn't earned the right to floss like that with me, though.

Since Shauna's graduation party, my club had become the spot in New York City. All the big name celebrities and rappers reserved their VIP tables on a weekly basis. Business was booming so much, we had to expand. We created a special VIP section for the top-notch celebrities who couldn't mingle with the regular public and the old

VIP section was reserved for B-list actors and rappers, people who at one point in their careers were at the top of their game, but were no longer as hot as they used to be. However, the public still yearned to see them. Therefore, they received special treatment at the club and that kept the gold diggers coming to the club on a weekly basis. There was a different group of groupies who frequented the club everyday of the week. On the night when most of the rappers came by the club, all the hoochie mamas with hopes of making it big with a rap star were in line waiting, wearing the shortest skirts and tightest outfits they could find in their closets. On the nights when the actors were around, we had every actor and actress wannabe in the club trying to get an audition. Some of them didn't mind auditioning in the club in front of everybody. While many of them took their craft seriously, there were many more willing to do anything just to get a cameo in a film.

It wasn't unusual for the actors and rappers to leave the club with three or four women at a time. It didn't take a genius to know that some of these women were willing to go to extreme measures to be seen with a famous person. Shauna was one of those women who went to those measures to be seen on the arm of a celebrity. She had ridden more limousines than Donald Trump had. The only difference was that she had seen more of the roofs of the limousines more than anything, because she was always laying on her back most of the time in the backseat. Shauna was the type of woman who liked to drop names of people she knew like the rest of the world cared. She had had breakfast with so many athletes, rappers and actors, I lost count. She honestly believed that I thought all she did was have breakfast with them. I still don't get why women think that rappers and actors are immune to talking about the women they bed. These guys talk more than regular guys because they have a lot more stories to tell.

Every man will gloat at one point or another, even if gloating could possibly jeopardize his family life. After all, most men are caught cheating because they cannot keep their big mouths shut about the women they're cheating with. They always feel that somebody needs to know their business. It could be a best friend, a brother or a cousin and when the story makes its way out or to a tabloid they want to act like they don't know how it was leaked.

Shauna was becoming a skank, but no one could tell her that she didn't have more class than the queen of England. She was giving up the goods like it was Christmas everyday and there were many takers. Shauna's arrogance was what tripped me out. She actually thought that she was the most irresistible woman to every man. I had already been there and done that and I was in love with Nia, so Shauna didn't stand a chance of getting back in my bed. Still, she thought she could and she tested her limits to the max.

There was the time when Shauna came to the club wearing this laced dress that hugged her body like I had never seen before. Through the material, it was easy to tell that she didn't have on any underwear. She paraded around the club that night like a tall glass of expensive champagne, but none of the ballers took her bait. I was actually laughing under my breath because Shauna looked like a high-class hooker. Any man with any kind of self worth would have stayed far away from her that night. She was just too obvious. After scouring the club without finding the type of man that she was looking for, her final destination was my office.

Shauna came in as I was handling my business and she started talking about how much she missed me. "You know what, Ron? I really miss you in my life. You and I used to have a lot of fun together and I always knew that some day you would be a success," she said. I did not know where she was going with her conversation, so I proceeded with caution. "Well, I don't have to be out of your life, you just need to recognize that I'm seriously involved with somebody right now and I don't want to cross that line." "What line?" She started to demonstrate. "You mean to tell me if I came around your desk and sat right in front of you and spread my legs open so you can get a whiff of that good pussy, you mean you would turn me down? I know Nia's shy looking ass don't put it on you like I can." I couldn't believe Shauna. She was sitting on my desk with her dress pulled up to her thighs and exposing her pussy all in my face and all over my paperwork. I would be lying if I said that my dick did not get hard at the site of her pink twat, but I showed control and composure.

"Whatever we had sexually was in the past, and I'm beyond all that physical shit right now. Pussy does not move me anymore. I am motivated by success and drive and Nia is the most driven woman that I have ever been with. And FYI: she's great in bed too." Shauna gave me this look like she didn't believe me. "If pussy doesn't motivate you, why is your dick so hard? Maybe pussy in general doesn't motivate you, but my pussy will always get a rise out of you. You remember that time when you and I went to the peep show in Manhattan and you started fucking me in that booth? I remember how you spread my legs open on that little stool and you started eating me so well. We had completely forgotten about the stripper in the booth as you and I started getting it on. My pussy was drenched with my juice as you ate me, my body started trembling. Then I took all ten inches of you in my mouth until you started begging me for mercy and that was also the first time that I ever swallowed any man's semen. The funny thing about that was that I never felt funny about doing it even though I initially thought it was nasty. Are you going to tell me that we didn't have a great time when we were together? You had me sitting on your dick in that little ass booth and you fucked me every which way until the stripper in the booth screamed that she wanted part of the action, remember?" "Yeah, I remember, but I also remember the times when you were chasing after the athletes because I couldn't afford to give you some of the things you wanted. I remember you losing your patience with me and telling me that I was not a baller. You've been with the ballers, how does it feel? I cannot go back to the past because Nia is my future and right now, you need to close your legs and pick up yourself and go home. I will always be here as a friend, but that's the extent of our relationship. I'm not gonna hurt Nia," I said firmly. I really did not want to embarrass Shauna further, but I had to be honest with her. Of course, she called me an asshole before leaving my office.

For consolation at the end of the night, she left with one of those washed up rappers who still had a few dollars left to buy a bottle of Moet in the club. That dude walked around with that bottle of Moet all night advertising to the world that he still had a couple of hundred dollars left from his rapping days. I caught a glimpse of them leaving in his 1990 BMW trying to hold on to his past fame.

Chapter 24
The Good Life

Everything in my life was going great. My business was booming, my woman was supportive and loving, and my parents were proud. I could not ask for anything more. I had been working so hard, I needed to take a quick vacation with Nia. She had not been properly rewarded for the hard work that she had put into my club and a quick weekend getaway to the Bahamas was just what the doctor ordered.

I had to make sure that my dad didn't mind looking after the club while I was gone for the weekend. He had been my right hand man in the day-to-day operations of the business from day one and he knew exactly what needed to be done in my absence. The employees knew that my father was an even tougher boss than I was, so I knew that they would all show up on time for work and do whatever my father needed them to do. My father was not shy about docking someone for five minutes off their pay if they were late. I know it sounds petty, but it was his way of making sure that the employees were disciplined enough to show up for work on time. There were times when I eased up a little with my employees and they tried to take advantage, but my father was always there to reinforce order.

After confirming with my dad that it was okay for me to go away for the weekend, I called the airline and I booked a roundtrip flight to Nassau in the Bahamas. I wanted to surprise Nia. I made all the arrangements to stay at the Atlantis resort and hotel on Paradise Island. I couldn't wait to surprise Nia with a short vacation. That day, I called to tell her that I was going to go to her house to chill with her because I missed her. I hadn't seen her in a couple of days and I couldn't go one more day without seeing her. Nia was starting to become my good habit and I wanted to indulge as much as possible.

One of the nicest things about my relationship with Nia was that we had a friendship that I felt was tighter than our intimate relationship. We were friends and lovers. I couldn't ask for anything more. She and I could talk about anything. We didn't have to have sex all the time when we were around each other. Sometimes, we just chilled in each other's arms in front of the television and that was enough. I'm not trying to downplay the fact that we had a lot of sex, but intimacy was primary in our relationship. The comfort that I felt in Nia's arms was enough for me to know that she was the woman that I wanted to be with for the rest of my life. I was looking forward to cuddling with her that night.

I arrived at Nia's house around nine o'clock. She greeted me at the door wearing a nice satin chemise and I could see the contour of her body wrapped by that fabric. I almost got a hard on instantly. To top it off, she was smiling from ear to ear and I could never get enough of her beautiful smile. Something about Nia's smile just made me want to smile. She brought joy to my life and I was happy with the little things that she did to make me feel special. That night, I was supposed to surprise Nia with my gift, but instead, it turned out that I got a surprise of my own. After taking off my jacket and hung it up in the closet in the foyer, I checked to make sure that the plane tickets were in my jacket pocket. As I followed Nia to the dining room, I could see the lights

126

were dimmed and I could smell the aroma of Shrimp Scampi coming from the kitchen. Nia had prepared a romantic dinner with wine and soft music. At the twist of her finger, I could hear Maxwell crooning "This Woman's Work" over the speakers.

She invited me into the dining room where she set the romantic mood with candles, soft music, great food and herself as my tasty dessert. It wasn't hard for me to work up an appetite. I watched Nia as she set the plates on the table and brought the food back and forth from the stove and the caring that went into her cooking and I knew that I wanted to get down on bended knee to ask her hand in marriage. However, I could not. I did not have a ring with me. What sense would it have made if I ask her to marry me without a ring in my hand? As we sat across from each other eating and having a light conversation about our day, Nia extended her leg across the table and ran her foot up and down my leg while winking her eyes and flirting with me. I was so happy with her flirtatious ways I told her "don't start nothing that you can't finish." "Why would I want to finish it? I want it to go on forever," she said. "What do you mean?" I asked. "I want us to never stop flirting and playing with each other and I don't ever want us to stop being intimate. Every time I see you, I want us to start something without ever finishing it. I want it to be something like the old Batman episodes. There will always be something to look forward to." "I like that," I answered.

As we continued to chow down on Shrimp Scampi, I kept staring at Nia and imagining our lives together. She definitely possessed the maternal instincts that I was looking for in a woman. I couldn't help comparing her to my mother. She was gracious, beautiful, smart and most of all supportive. "Life with this woman would be filled with joy and happiness," I thought to myself. Nia and I were taking turns watching each other without saying much. Each time I looked up, she looked down and each time she looked up, I looked down into my plate. The food in the plate was great to look at, but I enjoyed watching Nia a lot more.

"What would you say if I asked you to be my husband?" Nia asked out of the blue. "The honor would be all mine and you'd make me the happiest man on this earth," I said. "Well Ron, we've been together for a while now and I feel that we have the best chemistry that I have ever experienced and I know that I want to spend the rest of my life with you. You probably think that it's nontraditional for a woman to ask a man to marry her, but when we met you knew that I was not traditional. What I'm trying to say is – will you marry me?" She shocked the hell out of me with that one. I was hoping to have a big weekend in the Bahamas with her. My brother and I were making plans to go shopping for a ring for her, because I was planning to ask her to be my wife while we were in the Bahamas, but she beat me to it. The only thing I could say or do, at the time, was grab and pull her towards me for a long kiss. "Of course, I would marry you. I have wanted to make you my wife since the day you walked into the club. You are the best thing that has ever happened to me and there's no grass greener anywhere even if Martha Stewart herself grew it."

I was on a love high, so I carried Nia to the bed where I proceeded to gently kiss her and caress her body with my hands. I especially loved her round booty and as my hands wandered around her waist down to her butt, Nia pulled my belt off and unbuttoned my pants allowing them to drop to the floor. I was standing in front of her bed with my pants around my ankles and a huge bulge in my underwear. I kicked my shoes off before I jumped on the bed to join her and somehow I managed to finagle my pants off my ankle without using my hands. Nia was lying on her back as I kissed her from her forehead down to her lips. Her kisses had never felt more sensual than this moment. I could feel her hotness and wetness as she lifted her left leg across my right leg to get our bodies wrapped tightly while we engulfed in a passionate kiss. My hands made their way down to her breasts and I started caressing them like they were passion fruit from a West Indian garden. They had never been so tasty. Nia's passionate moaning fueled my energy to satisfy her need to climax. I licked my way down to her navel and she couldn't help holding on to my head because she knew that I would soon reach my destination between her legs and I would use my tongue as the accelerator to get her juices flowing.

Soon her clit was at the tip of my tongue; I could feel Nia's legs shaking uncontrollably; and I aimed to please her even more. As the sensual oral attack on her clitoris continued, she whispered to me "Ron, I want to make this pussy officially yours forever. I can't see myself doing this with anybody ever again. Please don't ever stop loving me." With a mouth full, I attempted to give her the best satisfying answer that I could come up with at the time "Baby, you taste so good, even if I was deaf, dumb and blind I wouldn't stop loving you. You are officially the end to my search for a life partner and I will never stop loving, eating, satisfying and pleasing you." All of that was said between laps of my tongue in and out of her. Just before I completed my sentence I heard a loud roar "I'm cumming, baby! You feel so good! Oh God I'm cumming!"

Nia was not the silent type. She wanted to let a brother know that she was satisfied and I knew that I was a master painter when it came to using my tongue like a paintbrush on a masterpiece. I sent Nia into another orgasmic convulsion and without notice, she wrapped her legs tight around my neck and exclaimed, "Baby, I'm cumming again, I'm cumming. You're making me cum again." For some reason, those words always satisfied my ego and I didn't want to stop hearing them, especially from Nia. She was also nothing to mess with in the bedroom. My baby had skills. After Nia got her nut off, it was her turn to return the favor. I brought my lips up to hers for another long kiss almost in a consoling way because I saw tears running down her face while she climaxed. We kissed passionately for about sixty seconds before Nia ordered me to lie down on my back. As I lay down on my back, Nia slowly made her way from my lips down to my chest kissing and licking every inch of my body. She skipped my crotch, went down to my knees, and started massaging them with her tongue. For some reason she knew how to make me weak in the knees, literally. I never knew I had a weakness in my knees until I met Nia. She licked and kissed my knees until I couldn't take it anymore. I had to beg for mercy and duly noted, she made her way back up to my crotch and before I knew it, she had my ten inches enveloped in her mouth.

The warmth of Nia's mouth around my dick forced me to tilt my head back towards the sky to thank the heavens above. However, I was looking to the sky for my own selfish pleasures and I wish that God would not strike me down as I enjoyed Nia's luscious lips maneuvering around my dick. When I felt Nia's smooth tongue twirling around the tip of my penis, all I could say to her was "Baby, don't stop. I don't ever want you to stop treating me this good." The motion of her hand at the base of my testicles forced me to grab on to the sheets on the bed as I pleaded for mercy. Nia did things to me that I could only appreciate with the woman I loved. I was in paradise as she worked her magic on me; stroking my manhood back and forth until I exploded all over her chest.

However, we were not done yet. The night was still young and we both had a lot of energy left. After regaining my full erection from my last nut, I asked Nia to get on me facing the wall so I could admire her beautiful, round booty riding me. She held on to my hands as she went up and down my dick and the vision of me going in and out of her got me even more excited. "Ooh baby, give it to me. You feel so good inside me, I don't want you to stop," she whispered. I did not want to stop either, but if she continued doing what she was doing, I would soon be busting another nut without much control. I had to regain control of the situation. I closed my eyes to imagine a soothing atmosphere with the most pleasant person that I could share it with in order to keep from cumming. I wanted to feel Nia's breath on me while I was inside of her.

I turned her around and had her lying on top of me so I could kiss her while making passionate love. As Nia started to grind on me, I held on to her body and with the rapid movement I could feel that she was about to cum yet again. I grabbed the back of her head, took her tongue inside my mouth, and continued to wind until I heard her scream, "Oh shit, this is good!" "It's good for me too, baby," I said as I finally allowed myself to cum along with her.

Later that night, Nia fell asleep in my arms and I watched her most of the night. Each time I woke up to look at her, I started smiling. I knew that Nia was the best thing that ever happened to me and I knew that I wanted to make sure she would never leave my side. Sometime during the night, I must've fallen asleep because I woke up the next morning to the smell of turkey bacon, eggs, English muffins and fresh squeezed orange juice. Nia was the total package, a great lover, a best friend, a great cook and sexy as hell.

Chapter 25
The Bahamas

Nia and I left for the Bahamas on a Friday morning. We slept through the whole plane ride to Nassau. When we landed, the misty island air hit us dead in the face and we instantly felt revived. The hotel offered a complimentary ride from the airport. The landscape of the island was beautiful as the driver took us through roundabouts and streets lined with vibrantly painted, luxury homes. However, when got to the hotel, they told us we couldn't check in until three o'clock that afternoon. We had arrived in Nassau at eleven o'clock in the morning. Therefore, that meant we had to find something to do or somewhere to go for four hours. Our mini vacation didn't have a good start. As we looked and asked around about what we could do around the island, we noticed that the Bahamian folks also weren't the friendliest. Everyone seemed to have an attitude for no reason at the hotel. The attitude and unfriendliness was restricted to the Nassau Beach hotel as we soon discovered that there were people on the island who enjoyed having the tourists there. The U.S dollar spoke volumes. After leaving our bags in a little special area with the bellhop and leaving a ten-dollar tip with him for watching our luggage, we were out the door to find something to do.

It wasn't hard to figure out that Nassau's economy relied heavily on tourism. Everyone we saw was visiting from a different place. We hardly ran into any locals doing any leisure activities. They were mostly working at the hotels or providing some other type of service that the tourists needed. Nia and I decided to go to the hotel next door to kill time at the casino. We were in there for a total of four hours and I was in the red for almost $300 dollars at the blackjack table. I was a little heated that I had lost my money so quickly, but I didn't want it to ruin my vacation. Nia was on the other side playing the slot machines and by the time she came back to get me, she was pronounced the grand prizewinner of $10,000 over the intercom. It was beginner's luck because Nia had never been in a casino in her life. The only reason she decided to play the slot machine was because she wanted something to do and the game only required her to feed quarters into the machine. The funny thing about it was that her luck started rubbing on me as well. With Nia standing besides me, I won all of my money back in a matter of thirty minutes. By the time I left the table a half hour later, I had won close to a $1000. I also increased my bets when I noticed that Nia was my good luck charm.

We left the casino with close to $15,000 between the two of us. Nia was happy that she had won the money and she decided to treat me to a nice Movado watch. We went into one of the shops and my eyes lit up when I saw the latest model of stainless steel Movado sitting in the display case. I always wanted a nice watch, but I never made it a priority. Nia must've been watching my face as I glanced at the watch because when I left to go to the shop next door, she decided to stay behind to look around a little longer. By the time we met around the corner fifteen minutes later, she had the watch gift-wrapped and surprised me with it. It was a nice gesture, but I had a little surprise of my own. It was something that I kept to myself until Nia and I got back to the States.

That weekend Nia and I had so much fun in the Bahamas. We went parasailing, deep sea diving and my favorite: jet skiing. We were in love and did not mind a little public display of affection every now and again. We also made love all over the room and at the beach. One night, Nia and I went down to the beach located behind the hotel and we decided to go skinny-dipping. It didn't take long for Nia and me to be wrapped up in each other's arms in the middle of the ocean. It was dark and quiet and the water was soothing. We were flirting and joking around and before I knew it, I found myself inside Nia with her legs wrapped around my waist. Being in the water made it easy for me to carry Nia and I was stroking and kissing her like we were on a private beach.

Nia's breasts a la salt water tasted so good. She was riding me like she was in a rodeo as I sucked on her breast. She held on to my neck with her head tilted back for a better affect. Nia's ass was kryptonite to me and as I reached to grab her beautiful ass, I heard her say to me "stroke me harder." And I did. I was stroking and stroking until my baby started screaming aloud. We could see a couple getting into the water butt naked getting ready to do what we were doing. Nia didn't care about them as she yelled, "Fuck me. Fuck me like I wanna be fucked." I obliged. I must've fucked Nia for a good half hour before we both finally came. It must've fueled the other couple who was about a hundred feet from us because I could hear the woman saying to her boyfriend "fuck me like he was fucking her." With that said, it was time for Nia and I to take our naked asses back to the room. We were laughing as we ran out of the water butt naked to retrieve our clothes. It was so dark I don't think the other couple was able to see our faces. We certainly couldn't tell who they were.

Overall, Nia and I had a great time in the Bahamas and we made plans to visit the island again in the future for a longer vacation. We went to Nassau and did many different tours around the island. We met folks who wanted to show us where to go to have fun, but we declined every time. Our goal was to spend time with each other and that's exactly what we did.

The evening we got back to New York, I wanted to reveal my surprise to Nia. After taking a shower with her and more sex in the shower, I decided it was time to make our engagement official. While Nia was sneaking around trying to surprise me with my favorite watch, I was at the jewelry store buying an engagement ring. We had seen this ring at the store where she bought the watch and I saw how her eyes lit up when she first noticed the ring, but the shop next door had the exact same ring for sale at a ten percent discounted price. I was able to pay cash for half the price of the ring and the other half I charged on my credit card. It was a two-carat princess cut diamond ring that was simple but the design was classy. I purchased the ring before I met up with Nia in the lobby. Since I was wearing shorts, I did not want her to get suspicious of the bulge that a jewelry box would create in my pocket. So, I took the ring out of the box, wrapped it in the receipt and the warranty papers, and stuck it in my underwear. My t-shirt was big enough to keep it from being conspicuous.

Before we went to bed that night after kissing Nia, I got on one knee and said to her, "Baby, I know that you asked me to marry you the other day and I was glad that you did. But today I want our engagement to be official." I pulled the ring out, extended my hand to Nia, and asked, "Will you make me the happiest man for the rest of my life?" My baby answered with a loud "yes" as tears streamed down her face. Nia was also surprised that I managed to buy the ring that she was crazy about. When she asked when and how I was able to do it, I simply answered, "Love has a way of bringing out the best in people and right now I feel that you have brought the best out in me and I wanted you to have the best, so I found a way." She was satisfied with my answer because she knew I wasn't going to reveal my secret.

Chapter 26
It's a Family Affair

I never made a habit of bringing women home to meet my parents, but when we came back from the Bahamas I decided to tell them about Nia and my mom was surprised. My dad had seen Nia around the club a couple of times and he took notice of the affect that she had on me. My mom, however, was a hard sell. It was hard for my mother to buy into the fact that I had fallen in love with a woman. While visiting my mother the Friday before Easter Sunday, I told her that I wanted to invite a special friend to church with us and to also join us for dinner afterwards. "I know you're not thinking of bringing that high yellow girl Shauna to my church," my mom exclaimed. "Shauna? Why would you think that I wanted to bring Shauna to church with me?" "Ronny, you don't think I see how that high yellow girl got your nose wide open? She's beautiful and all, but there's something stink about her and I don't want to see you hurt, son," she said. "Thanks for your concern, mom, but I was not talking about Shauna. I'm talking about my girlfriend…. Excuse me, my fiancée, Nia." She reacted, "Fiancée? When did this all happen? Boy, you jump from one thing to the next without thinking and now you're talking about some damn fiancée." "Mom, I'm serious. This is the woman that I really love and we got engaged while were in the Bahamas." "Boy, you done lost your mind. Is she another high yellow girl with long hair? I am tired of you young men getting whipped by these no good women who have nothing to offer but beauty. Why don't you find a nice girl like your brother?" I knew I had to change the topic once my mom brought my brother's wife into the conversation.

The whole time my mom and I were talking, my dad never said a word. He sat back grinning, allowing my mom to grill me. He knew damn well that I was not talking about Shauna, but he never came to my defense. "Why don't we just wait until you meet her then you can form an opinion of her. I'm not gonna tell you anything more about her, but you need to let go of your preconceived notions of her," I said to my mom. "Son, are you happy? As long as you're happy that's all I care about. I don't want no hussy hurting my baby," she said while pulling on my cheeks. My mom always treated me like a baby. Sometimes I enjoy it and sometimes I don't, but what can I say? She's my mom and I love her to death.

I had no worries because I knew my woman could handle her own. "If my mother thought my brother's wife was special, wait till she meets Nia," I thought to myself. I was anticipating the day when my whole family would finally get to meet my future wife. I got to Nia's apartment later that evening anxious to tell her about coming to Easter service with my family. She already knew my dad, but never met my mom. Nia thought my dad was cool and down to earth, so she assumed my mother had to be somewhat of a cool person in order for my dad to have married her.

"Baby, you know I told my mom about our engagement today." "You did? That's good I'll finally get a chance to meet the woman who raised such a fine young man," she said. "I told her she was gonna love you and that you make me the happiest man on earth." "I hope so, because I've been the happiest woman ever since I met you," she responded. Ever since I got engaged to Nia, all I could think about was the wonderful life ahead of us. We never as much had a major argument since we've been together. This was the woman of my dreams and nothing was gonna keep us apart. Well, that's what I thought until Shauna called to give me the worst news that a person could receive from anybody.

The dinner at my parents' house went well. Everyone was impressed with Nia, including my brother's wife. She had finally started to notice my maturity and she congratulated me for making such a great choice in a woman. My mother and Nia cozied up very quickly and they spent most of the evening talking to and laughing with each other. My dad knew Nia, but he had no idea that she was as great a person as she displayed that evening. Everyone was having a great time except me. Shauna's phone call had changed my mood and I couldn't let go of the fact that she said to me, "We need to talk. I'm in the hospital and it's important that you get here as soon as possible."

The first thing that ran through my mind was that time that I slipped up and had sex with Shauna one last time before I totally committed to Nia. It was a few months ago and I wondered if there was a possible pregnancy as a result. Shauna wouldn't confirm nor deny my suspicions over the phone. I wish she had called me a couple of days earlier and not a couple of hours before I had to pick up Nia for the dinner at my parents' house. My stomach was turning because all I could think about during dinner was the fact that Shauna was about to ruin what I had with Nia, the woman I loved.

After dinner, my family decided to play Scrabble and Spades for a few hours in the family room and I could tell that everyone was genuinely falling in love with Nia. I imagined that it wasn't going to be that hard for my family to love her because she was a great person anyway. I was bothered, but I hid it well. All I could think about was Nia's reaction when she finds out that I got Shauna pregnant while I was dating her. I was already playing in my head the reverse psychology that I was going to use to secure her forgiveness. I could use the fact that we hadn't officially spoken about the full nature of our relationship and therefore that left the door open for me to do what I wanted. Or I could simply own up to the fact that I was horny that night and Shauna came in wearing a skimpy dress and she somehow managed to slip and fall on my dick. For some reason I didn't think Nia would buy the latter.

Usually I'm good at Scrabble and only my brother is usually better than me, but that night I couldn't think of the most basic words. Shauna's situation dominated my thoughts and I was about to lose the best thing that ever happened to me. Even the afterthought of making love to Nia when we got to her house later that evening didn't appeal to me. I knew that I couldn't be myself with her that night.

Finally, my parents decided to call it a night at midnight. Everybody hugged and kissed and my parents handed their home number to Nia and told her not to be a stranger. My mother wanted to play a significant role in helping to plan our wedding. I was thinking that there might not be a wedding at all.

Chapter 27
The Long Ride Home

After leaving my parents' house, I drove Nia home and I didn't say too much in the car on the way there. She could sense that something was bothering me. "You know, I've noticed that you haven't been yourself all night. Is something bothering you? Are you having second thoughts about our engagement, because if you are, we can call it off until you're ready," she said. I wanted to take the opportunity to tell her "hell no! I'm not ready." But deep in my heart, I was ready than ever. Nia completed me and I enjoyed that feeling. I tried as much as I could to look her straight in the eye to tell her the best possible lie that I could come up with. "Nia, how could you think that I'm not ready? I'm trying my best to put forth the effort to make this thing work between us and already you're having your doubts. You know that I don't like to be doubted and if you feel like that, maybe you're insecure about our relationship." I crossed my finger and hoped that reverse psychology bullshit I unloaded on her would work. However, I was dealing with a compassionate woman who appreciated a good man. "Baby, I do not doubt our relationship. I just want to make sure that we are ready for our future together. You are everything I have ever wanted in a partner, friend and husband and I just want to make sure that you are happy." She fucked me up with that one. There was no way I could say anything hurtful to her. It was time to switch up.

I knew that Nia was in my corner and I needed her there and I wanted to keep her at all cost. The next best thing was to try to buy time so I could resolve the issues

142

between Shauna and me. I knew if Shauna was pregnant she would want to keep the baby out of spite and not love for that child. Shauna had a problem with the fact that I treated Nia like a princess and I knew that she would try to do anything in her power to destroy my relationship with Nia.

My mama always told me that I was the best lying son that she ever had because I was always quick on my feet when I needed to think of ways to get out of situations. That was also one of the reasons why my daddy almost wore out my backside as a little boy. My father thought that he had beaten the habit out of me as a little boy, but a little part of it still lived within me and I needed to use it to buy time so I can fix my relationship with Nia. The nightclub was my perfect opportunity and excuse. "Baby, I've been under a lot of stress lately because I'm putting together this party for this corporation and the lady that I'm working with is really difficult." It wasn't a total lie because I was really hosting this party at my club, but everything was going according to plan. I knew that Nia was going to offer her help, that's why I told her about this difficult party-planner hired by the corporation that I was working with. "You know I'm used to doing things my way, but I couldn't pass up this opportunity because these people are paying a lot of money to have their party at my club," I told her. "Don't let it consume you. It's only a party," she assured me.

By the time I reached Nia's house, my excuse was good enough for her to let me go home and be by my lonesome. I told her that I needed to come up with the party favors and make up a list of hired help hat I needed to serve the guests all night. And just like that I was off the hook. I gave my baby a long kiss goodnight and I was on my way to deal with the real reason why my stomach was in a notch all night. That fucking Shauna wanted to destroy something that I treasured and there was no way I was gonna let that happen.

After dropping Nia off, I picked up my phone and called Shauna. I didn't give a damn how late it was. This chick was gonna hear from me. The phone rang once and went straight to voicemail. I dialed again and the same shit happened. I was going out of my mind wondering why she wasn't picking up her phone. Shauna was not the type to ignore my calls or shut off her phone at night. "What the hell could be wrong with her?" I wondered. My mind was all over the place because I hadn't a clue what could be wrong with Shauna.

Chapter 28
A Restless Night

I made it home in no time. I wanted to take my clothes off and fall right to sleep, but I couldn't. I tossed and turned until about three in the morning, and just when I was able to finally drift away to sleep, I started having this dream that was more like a nightmare.

I was dressed in a black tuxedo and I was in this big church standing in front of this minister with my bride standing across from me. As the minister announced the vows, I started to pull the veil off my future wife's face and it was none other than Shauna. She was standing before me looking sickly with sores all over her face and her beauty had completely faded away. When the minister finally said, "you may kiss the bride," I went to kiss Shauna and her lips were crackling and bleeding. She had sores all over her mouth and a group of men were in the background yelling to me one by one, "I wouldn't do that if I were you." "Those lips have sucked more dicks than a porno star," yelled another. "My brother and I had a threesome with her," yelled this man dressed in baggy jeans sagging over his ass in a tank top with a bandana around his head like a rapper. "The whole team had a piece of that," screamed another man dressed like a football player wearing a helmet. The room started spinning and Shauna was looking scarier and scarier each time I looked at her.

"You might as well kiss her now because everyone else had a piece, including me," said the minister while laughing. "Congratulations, someone had to marry Ms. Door Knob. Everybody had a turn." I wanted to run to every one of those men and punch each of them in the face, including the minister, but for some reason I had no strength and I could not move my legs and arms. It was as if I was paralyzed.

I woke up with sweat beads trickling down my face and I didn't want to go back to sleep. I was trying to figure out why Shauna was in my dream and the significance of everything that happened in it. I was a little scared, but I didn't know what to do. Sometime during the night I drifted off to sleep again only to be awakened a short while later by my alarm, which was set for eight o'clock in the morning. On the nights when I didn't work at the club, I usually woke up early to go to the gym to work out. However, I was too drained to work on anything that morning. The only thing I wanted to do was to speak to Shauna.

Chapter 29
A Hard Unexpected Curve Ball

When I woke up, the first thing I wanted to do was to find out what was up with Shauna. That chick had me tripping over a situation that I wasn't even sure existed. It could have all been in my head because I was paranoid. However, my paranoia would soon disappear with the reality of the worse possible news that I could've received from Shauna. My hands were shaking as I picked up the phone to dial her number. The phone rang once and then twice confirming the fact that she had it turned on. By the third ring, I was anticipating Shauna's voice on the other end, but instead, I heard a man's voice on her phone. My first thought was "she found the real father of her child," but that wasn't the case. A male nurse from SUNY Downstate Medical Center in Brooklyn picked up the phone. "Hello this is Nurse Michael Carrington, are you a kin of Ms. Williams?" "No, I'm actually a friend and I'm calling to make sure she's okay." He answered, "Well, it all depends on what you call okay. Has Ms. Williams revealed her condition to you sir?" "What condition? What the hell are you talking about?" I screamed through the phone. "Sir, you're gonna have to call back because Ms. Williams is a bit tired and she's asleep right now." "Before you hang up can you please tell me what room she's in?" He told me the room number and how to get to the hospital.

I was still in a paranoid state as I jumped in the shower to clean up so I could head to the hospital to see Shauna. I needed to get to the bottom of the situation. I hopped in my car and made it to the hospital in no time even with the countless gypsy cabs and dollar vans crowding the streets of Brooklyn. After I reached the hospital, I told the receptionist that I was there to visit Shauna Williams and she simply directed me to her floor. The first thing I noticed was that she was not housed in the maternity ward. So that eased my tension a little bit and I felt that perhaps she wasn't pregnant. Looking back on it now, pregnancy should've been the least of my worries.

When I finally made it to Shauna's room, the first thing I saw was the noticeable excess weight loss on her. Then I noticed the appearance of discolored, purplish growths on her skin, skin rashes, and a thick whitish coating on her mouth. I almost vomited because the Shauna I knew didn't look like that. I was worried because she seemed all but gone. She was hardly alert when she opened her eyes to see me standing by her bed. She tried to reach for my hand, but I pulled back because I didn't know if the sores on her body were contagious. Beautiful Shauna had turned into somewhat of a monster. It had only been nine months since I last saw her. Shauna also noticed my reaction to her as well and I could hear her whisper with the little strength she had left, "I don't know what you're afraid of because you might have it too." I had an Arnold from Different Strokes episode when I said to her, "what you talking about Shauna?" She wasn't in the best physical shape to answer me, but her male nurse came back in the room and she shook her head to give him the okay to tell me that she had fallen victim to the HIV virus. My heart almost hit the floor as Michael revealed to me that Shauna was hospitalized because she was in the wasting stages of AIDS where the body's organs can no longer function at full capacity.

148

Apparently, Shauna had gone to the emergency room to get treated for a cold that she thought was lasting too long and that's when she discovered that she had developed full-blown AIDS. She had no idea whom she might've caught the HIV virus from and the reason for her calling me was to inform me that I needed to get tested. Forget paranoia, now I had this cloud of this disease riding over my head and I knew that it was very possible that I could've been HIV positive because I had sex with Shauna without using protection on more than one occasion. Not only that, I was also worried that Nia's life might be destroyed as well because of me. Scared is not a strong enough word to describe how I was feeling. But first, I was angry. I was angry enough to wrap my hands around Shauna's throat and wring her neck.

I was also angry for allowing myself to get caught up in that situation. I never cared enough about myself as a person to protect myself from possible sexually transmitted diseases from the women that I was sleeping with. Shauna wasn't the only woman that I slept with unprotected. There were many others and only the Lord knew how many of them I could've infected if I indeed carried that disease. Like most victims of HIV, I allowed my preconceived notions about the disease to cloud my judgment. I thought that only avid drug users, homosexuals and women that appeared to be promiscuous carried the disease, but I should have known better.

Chapter 30
HIV and AIDS

Watching Shauna in the hospital nearing her death brought me back to my college days when one of my college professors who was an AIDS activist, brought a guest speaker to speak with us about the disease. It was not the type of lecture that students or people were used to. This man was a former CIA agent who was on a mission to clear his conscience. He is no longer alive today, because of circumstances beyond his control, but I had a chance to hear him tell us about the origination of AIDS.

For years, I refused to believe anything that man was saying about AIDS and how the US government was behind it. The white students were completely naive to the idea that the government could have possibly had a hand in the creation of AIDS. I was as well, but part of me wanted to believe that it was possible. However, since I never met or knew anyone that succumbed to the disease, I did not allow it to be a part of my daily thoughts. I was like most Americans, as long as I was not affected directly, who gave a damn.

The interesting thing that we learned that day in the classroom was probably the most important lesson that any student at any university could have learned. Our guest speaker was not shy about the fact that he could not stand George Herbert Walker Bush. According to him, it was under his leadership as Director of the Central Intelligence Agency (CIA) that the army was commissioned to create a disease in the lab for depopulation. The target groups were none other than the

Africans, Asians, Indians and the homosexual population in America. The implementation of this disease was actually reminiscent of the days when Black men were purposely injected with syphilis. However, the HIV virus would prove easier to administer because the US government went under the false pretense of crusaders to Africa, India and other third world countries and offered the poor people a free cure for tuberculosis. According to our guest speaker, these people viewed it as a gift from above, because they were being vaccinated for no charge against a disease that could potentially take their lives.

Millions of people lined up, and one by one, they were unknowingly injected with the HIV virus. The disease was especially created to destroy the immune system and would slowly die from it as it weakens the organs. Moreover, the fastest way to spread it was through sexual intercourse. The other way it could be spread was blood transfusion. Now that I am older, I could see the logic behind it. Almost all humans want to have sex at one point in their lives and if people are susceptible to this disease when they have sex, it was the perfect weapon for depopulation. There was a lot that I did not decipher as a youngster, but as people get into situations they start to think about things and life differently.

As I continued to stare at Shauna, a lot of what that man was saying to us that day started coming back to me. Most people never questioned the fact that AIDS suddenly came out of nowhere, and most of the people being blamed for the disease were of African descent, initially. The theory that it came from monkeys from Africa was widely accepted, but I started asking myself, "how had these Africans been living with these monkeys for so many years and never acquired this disease before?" No one in Africa was dying of AIDS. What George Bush didn't think about while he was planning to annihilate a whole race of people, was the fact that White people or tourists in general sometimes fall in love with the natives of the places they visit. And that sometimes leads to sex and if this disease is transmitted through sex, the chances of an American tourist bringing it back to America was very likely and now America has a crisis in its hands, but we all know who's affected the most. Even with Bush's plan to target homosexuals, he failed. It does not take a genius to know that the Bush family and most of the politicians in Washington D.C. are not the brightest people around. They never once realized that not every person who sleeps with men is homosexual. Some of them are also bisexual. So, this disease has become a mainstream crisis for the world, but the root of it seemed to have been forgotten by all of the scientists. Perhaps the reason could be because they created it and they don't want to reveal that.

We were also told that most diseases are researched until concrete evidence for its origination or source is found, but somehow society has managed to sell their African monkey theory to the world. They even started to blame it on the small island of Haiti at one time. Some of us were ignorant enough to believe that this disease could've come from the island. Black folks seem to always live up to the ignorance that they expect from us and I, too, was ignorant at one point in my life. If Bush and his goons were looking for a way to depopulate...mission accomplished. I hope that one day an investigation will lead to his involvement of this genocide and he will go down in history, making Hitler look like an angel. I am sure that time will prove that he was solely responsible for the new African Holocaust.

My research on AIDS led me to do a little research on the Bush family. I found that hatred, prejudice and racism are deeply rooted in the Bush family. The grandfather helped finance the Nazis in Germany during the Holocaust. Every member of that family since has been responsible for the mass murder of people of color in different parts of the world. They killed a bunch of Iraqis without proof that Saddam had any nuclear weapons or connections to Al Qaeda.   Nonchalant has always been their attitude and approach, but if there's truly a hell, they will all rot in it while hiding behind their fake belief in God. The President of the United States attacked a country based on one man's lie – a lie that was substantiated by other notable people who worked with him briefly. If 60 Minutes could find out the truth about this man, why couldn't the CIA? That wasn't even repulsive enough to me, because most leaders of the world are sinister in one way or another. However, what I found completely repulsive was the notion that this disease was tested on the homeless before it was administered on folks in the world, according to our guest speaker.

The basic reason behind it was simple. Who's going to report a homeless person missing?   Homeless people were rounded up at night and taken to labs to become guinea pigs for the creation of this deadly disease. That ultimately led to the destruction of millions of people in the world, similar to how the Black men in Tuskegee, Alabama were victimized. Everything about science has to be proven and these people were monitored for years to ensure that the virus actually worked. In order to find out if something can be proven, it has to be administered. We've seen this in the movies all the time, but most people fail to see the underlying messages in these films. The Matrix was the most powerful movie that ever came out of Hollywood, but most of us only found entertainment in it. The ideas for these, most of the time, is not all imagination. There's always some truth to what a writer writes.

Chapter 31
Denial

As I stood by Shauna's bedside watching how her beauty has deteriorated to nothing, I started to deny the possibility that I could be infected with this deadly disease. I wanted to continue to lead a normal life and act like I wasn't affected by Shauna's condition, but I couldn't. Every time I got around Nia, I was afraid to touch her. I didn't want her to catch anything from me and every little cough sent me panicking. I started to do research on HIV and AIDS without ever mentioning anything to Nia. I wanted to find out the early symptoms of HIV and through my research online and at the library, I learned about the following HIV/AIDS symptoms:

- Lack of energy

- Weight loss

- Frequent fevers and sweats

- A thick, whitish coating of the tongue or mouth that is caused by a yeast infection and sometimes accompanied by a sore throat

- Severe or recurring vaginal yeast infections

- Chronic pelvic inflammatory disease or severe and frequent infections like herpes zoster

- Periods of extreme and unexplained fatigue that may be combined with headaches, lightheadedness, and/or dizziness

155

- Rapid loss of more than ten pounds of weight that is not due to increased physical exercise or dieting

- Bruising more easier than normal

- Memory loss

- Long-lasting bouts of diarrhea

- Swelling or hardening of glands located in the throat, armpit, or groin

- Periods of continued, deep, dry coughing

- Increased shortness of breath

- The appearance of discolored or purplish growths on the skin or inside the mouth

- Unexplained bleeding from growths on the skin, from mucous membranes, or from any opening in the body

- Recurring or unusual skin rashes

- Severe numbness or pain in the hands or feet, the loss of muscle control and reflex, paralysis or loss of muscular strength

- An altered state of consciousness, personality change, or mental deterioration

- Children may grow slowly or fall sick frequently. HIV positive persons are also found to be more vulnerable to some forms of cancers.

Since I did not exhibit or experience any of these symptoms, I believed that I was spared from this deadly disease. I also buried myself in my work to get my mind off the situation. I felt fine and I looked well, so there was no way that I could be HIV positive. I think I wanted to convince myself more than anything.

While I was in denial and lying to myself, I was also trying my best to act normal with Nia. However, she was a smart woman and my constant negative reactions to her sexual advances were forcing her to believe that I was going out on her. I always used the lame excuse that I was too tired to have sex. Nia and I had also stopped using protection all together because she had gotten on the pill. I would not have been able to explain to her my sudden requirement to wear a condom during sex, especially since I was the one who insisted she got on the pill.

I wanted so much to talk to somebody about my situation, but I did not want my secret to get out. I did not want anybody to act prejudice towards me. Most people, whether we want to admit or not, are not receptive to HIV positive folks. As a society, we tend to frown on the sick, especially people with AIDS. We act like they are walking around spreading their germs around and if we as much breathe the same air as them we would get sick as well. I am not even ashamed to admit that I felt that way around Shauna. I did not even want to touch her and she was a woman that I could not keep my hands off at one time.

My denial period would last almost a month before I decided to go speak with a counselor about my possible

157

risk. I never touched Nia during that whole period and her suspicion of my infidelity grew. Honestly, I didn't even like the site of women at that time. Meanwhile, Shauna's health continued to deteriorate and I went to the hospital everyday to see her. I still felt connected to her and each time I went to the hospital, I kept telling her that she was going to beat the disease. I tried keeping her spirit up by talking about the good times we used to have. Every now and then, I could see a little smirk on her face.

Shauna was ashamed of the disease, so only her mother and I visited with her. She did not even tell Chenille about it. They were starting to grow apart anyway. Chenille was trying to focus on settling down with Myles while Shauna was still having her fun. Shauna's illness was our little secret and that's exactly how I wanted it. My family did not know, my friends did not know and I did not have to worry about people talking about me after I left a room. That was the ultimate fear. I didn't fear death; I feared living in this society with this deadly disease. There are people out there who wish that all AIDS patients could be quarantined and they have no problem showing their ignorance.

Chapter 32
Accepting Responsibility

It took me a while to finally come to grip with the reality that I was facing. I became withdrawn and I was starting to lose the most important person in my life, which was Nia. I really didn't want to hurt her and the only way to be certain that Nia was not at risk was for me to make sure that I wasn't already infected. And if I were infected, my plans were to tell Nia immediately before I killed myself. Oh, yes! I started experiencing suicidal ideation after I saw Shauna at the hospital. My plan was to swallow a bottle of Midol with an eighty proof bottle of vodka to make all problems disappear. I didn't want to live with the shame of AIDS. I wasn't educated enough to know that it was not a shame. The more I thought about killing myself, the more I realized I was being selfish. I thought about what if Nia is positive, who was going to be her pillar of strength? I also thought about the fact that she would hate me with a passion as well, just like I hated Shauna at first. However, I overcame my hatred for Shauna because she was not fully to blame for my erratic behavior. I was just as responsible and Nia would be accountable for her negligence as well, but I would still feel responsible for infecting her.

It was easy for me to blame Shauna because I had seen the many men that I thought she was sleeping with almost on a weekly basis. She always denied that she slept with any of them and I never believed her anyway. Now that she contracted AIDS, she confirmed my suspicions of her. That was only one side of it. I was also bringing home a different female every other night and never did I think about the risks involved. Yes, I used condoms occasionally when I felt that I did not trust a particular woman, but the fact of the matter remained that I did not practice safe sex one hundred percent of the time. It only takes one time to catch the disease.

I was also worried that I could have been the one to infect Shauna with this disease, because through my research I also discovered that some people could live symptom-free for as long as ten years during the asymptomatic period, while others may begin to have symptoms as soon as a few months. I was the athletic type, never been hospitalized or medicated for anything, so my immune system was strong.   Some of us walk around feeling invincible when we're young. This untouchable feeling is usually what leads to our downfall. I felt I was immune to AIDS because most of the women that I was messing with were college educated, professional, beautiful, and most importantly drug free. I couldn't be more wrong. I learned that everyone is susceptible to this disease, including my Viagra popping grandfather.

Now that I had accepted responsibility for my possible part in possibly contracting the disease, the next step was for me to get a diagnosis to confirm that I was an actual carrier. That's where I needed help. I wasn't going to just drive myself to the hospital and tell them that I wanted to be tested for AIDS. It wasn't as simple as that. My state of mind was not at ease like that. Only a counselor could help me come to grip with the reality of this disease and that's why I anonymously called the Brooklyn Psychotherapy Center and asked to speak to a counselor.

Chapter 33
Taking the Right Steps to Do the Right Thing

After speaking with this counselor at the Brooklyn Psychotherapy Center for a few minutes on the phone, she could sense that I was apprehensive about the whole thing, but she made me feel comfortable enough to schedule an appointment to see her at her office.

The whole point of my meeting with the HIV counselor was to educate me about testing. I always thought that HIV testing was something that was done n a small room with a phlebotomist drawing blood and a few minutes later a doctor in a white coat comes out to tell someone that they are HIV positive. It wasn't at all what I perceived.   So first, I had to be educated on HIV diagnosis and the counselor had many pamphlets and leaflets that gave me all the information that I needed.

She began, *"In the early stages of infection, HIV often causes no symptoms and the infection can be diagnosed only by testing a person's blood. Two tests are available to diagnose HIV infection - one that looks for the presence of antibodies produced by the body in response to HIV and the other that looks for the virus itself. Antibodies are proteins produced by the body whenever a disease threatens it. When the body is infected with HIV, it produces antibodies specific to HIV. The first test, called ELISA (Enzyme Linked Immunosorbent Assay), looks for such antibodies in blood. If antibodies are present, the test gives a positive result. A positive test has to be confirmed by another test called Western Blot or Immunoflouroscent Assay (IFA). All positive* tests by *ELISA* need not be accurate and hence Western Blot and repeated tests are necessary to confirm a person's *HIV* status. A person infected with *HIV* is termed *HIV-positive or seropositive.*" I just sat there and listened as she continued. "*As ELISA requires specialized equipment, blood samples need to be sent to a laboratory and the result will be available only after several days or weeks. To cut short this waiting period, RAPID TEST that gives results in 5 to 30 minutes, are increasingly being used around the world. The accuracy of rapid tests is stated to be as good as that of ELISA. Though rapid tests are more expensive, researchers have found them to be more cost effective in terms of the number of people covered and the time the tests take.*" "Interesting, I have options." "There are always options," she answered. "*The HIV- antibodies generally do not reach detectable levels in the blood until approximately three months after infection. This period, from the time of infection until the blood is tested positive for antibodies, is called the Window Period. Some times, the antibodies might take even six months to show up. Even if the tests are negative, during the Window Period, the amount of virus is very high in an infected person. Hence, if a person is newly infected, the risk of transmission is higher.*"

"I find your information to be very educational. How come they don't offer these things as workshops to high school students in New York City?" I asked. "Well, you'll have to talk to the mayor who continues to tell us that there's no money in the budget for such programs.

162

The number of infected high school students will continue to climb because of lack of education," she answered. "I damn sure could have used a workshop on HIV and AIDS when I was in high school," I answered. "There's more information that I need to go over with you, so just give me a few minutes then we can discuss what the City of New York can do for its students. Lord knows they're not doing enough." I allowed her to continue. *"If a person is highly likely to be infected with HIV and yet both the tests are negative, a doctor may suggest a repetition of the tests after three months or six months when the antibodies are more likely to have developed. The second test is called PCR (Polymerase Chain Reaction), which looks for HIV itself in the blood. This test, which recognizes the presence of the virus' genetic material in the blood, can detect the virus within a few days of infection. There are also tests like Radio Immuno Precipitation Assay (RIPA), a confirmatory blood test that may be used when antibody levels are difficult to detect or when Western Blot test results are uncertain. Other available tests are Rapid Latex Agglutination Assay, a simplified, inexpensive blood test that may prove useful in medically disadvantaged areas where there is a high prevalence of HIV infection, and p24 Antigen Capture Assay."*

I received a serious education and I wondered why I waited so long to learn everything that I needed to learn about HIV and AIDS. I guess most of us don't feel the need to educate ourselves about certain diseases unless it has hit home. I was grateful that the counselor was able to meet with me on such short notice and my next plan was to head to the Brownsville Multi-Service Family Health Center in Brooklyn to get myself tested.

The people at the center assured me that the test was being administered in strict confidence and that I would be contacted in a couple of weeks with the results. They also provided counseling as well as medical care in case my test came back positive. They also mentioned that family notification was available as well, but I wanted to be the one to tell my family if I was HIV positive. There was no way I was going to let some staff person from a clinic call my mom and dad to tell them that I was HIV positive.

To put my mind at ease, the counselor also told me about the different treatment options available for HIV and AIDS. "We all know that back in the day people seldom lived past five years after developing AIDS, but things are different and progress towards a so-called "cure" has been made." What she should have really told me was that the antidote for the disease was created at the same time the disease was created, but I can't blame her for not knowing.

In the past, I would have never believed that the government would create a disease to kill people, but not anymore. The US government's capabilities are substantial and while they have done some good deeds, they've also done twice as many evil deeds. The amount of money that the pharmaceutical companies and the US government benefit from AIDS research and medications is in the trillions. People continue to donate money to research something that's already known. According to the guest speaker at my university, the microbes found in the HIV virus came from sheep and cows, but we'll never hear that from any scientist because all the superpowers were behind this disease. The US Government works in accord with the other industrialized countries of the world, which are comprised of the United Kingdom, France, Germany and Spain.

"Till today, there is no conclusive treatment to eliminate HIV from the body; however, timely treatment of opportunistic infections can keep one healthy for many years. The commonly available treatment for AIDS is the treatment against opportunistic infections. Normally standard treatment regimens, used against such infections in non-HIV patients, also work well with the HIV-positive persons. If properly treated, almost all the opportunistic infections can be contained.

However, during the last decade, researchers have developed powerful drugs that check the replication of the virus at various levels. Called antiretroviral drugs, they are available in three classes and under various brands. Taken in combinations (called cocktail or combination therapy) under specialized medical advice, these drugs drastically reduce the viral load in blood. However, they do not permanently cure one of HIV. This line of treatment, called HAART (Highly Active Antiretroviral Therapy) has resulted in a huge reduction of AIDS-related deaths. Though many positive persons and caregivers have welcomed these drugs, others have experienced serious side effects. They are also very expensive and are out of reach for a majority of the infected people. But of late, the prices have been steeply falling," she informed me. At least she gave me hope.

Chapter 34
Impatiently Waiting

I may have been angry that this disease affected someone that I knew personally, and could possibly harm me, but I was no fool to go around telling people about what I had learned about HIV and AIDS back in college. Our guest speaker mysteriously died as he was making his way around the country to let his voice be heard, and I damn sure wasn't ready to mysteriously disappear or die. Shoot! I was afraid that AIDS might kill me and I was scared. Imagine the fear that I had in my mind for the government? Negroes like me who think they know too much usually don't live too long.

This government has a way of making people disappear when their viewpoint is not shared or their dirty deeds are exposed. I knew I couldn't take on the US government so I kept my mouth shut. What's the point of educating people when the government has done such a great job of withholding information and hiding the true facts? Most Americans would find that man's info about the US government regarding AIDS too far fetched to believe. However, the same government has openly admitted to the failed attempted assassination of Fidel Castro, the president of Cuba, just because they disagree with his views regarding communism. How exactly has Castro's views affected the lives of Americans? Somebody wanted him dead, though. Just like millions of Africans, Indians and Asians had to die.

While I impatiently awaited my fate, I wanted to make sure that I didn't sexually jeopardize Nia's life. I managed to avoid seeing her while I was going through

167

that turbulent period early on, but it was getting harder and harder to convince Nia that I was that busy at work. Nia enjoyed sex with me a whole lot as did I and I had better start serving up the goods before the suspicions of infidelity started to surface. A good ole cold could keep the lady away for a few days, so I started acting like I had a serious cold whenever we talked on the phone. Nia offered to come to my house to take care me, but I was too slick. "What's the point of both of us getting sick? It's just a cold and it'll go away after a couple of days and I could see you then," I said to her after she offered to help take care of me. "You know I feel real bad leaving you to deal with this cold by yourself. I want to take care of my baby," she replied. I can dish out the mushy stuff just as much as she could. "Your baby wants you to take care of him too, but I love my baby too much to let her get sick because I'm sick. I want my baby to be healthy so I can get some of that good loving after my recovery," I told her. I said I was good, didn't I? Nia could only respond with "your baby will be here waiting for you. Make sure you get a lot of rest and I'll call you everyday until you get better." And that she did. Nia called me so much, I felt smothered. I took it like a champ, because it kept her physically away from me.

Five days went by and I was still trying to ride the cold that I lied to Nia about. I got a feeling she was getting worried and would soon pay me a visit. I decided to call her to tell her that I was feeling better and the cold was completely gone. I didn't want my lies to start catching up to me. Nia also wanted to see me as soon as she could because I was now cured. I wanted to see her just as much as she wanted to see me, but I didn't know how to avoid making love to her. Just as luck would have it, my old roommate from college called me to see if he could come to New York to spend a week at my house. That was my way out of not seeing Nia for a while.

I went to Nia's apartment late that evening acting like I was exhausted from work. She knew that I had no energy to make love to her and I acted as if I wanted to just fall asleep. It was a lot of acting on my part because when Nia opened the door, she was wearing a nice pair of pink boy shorts with a matching bra. Her ass never looked so good and I fought my erection extremely hard. I wanted to jump my baby's bones, but not willing to risk exposing her to some deadly virus. I plopped my head into the soft pillow on her bed and commenced the fake snoring before she even got a chance to kiss or say anything to me. I didn't even bother getting undressed, but I could always rely on my baby to take care of me. She somehow managed to take my clothes off through my fake sleeping. I felt kind of bad because I knew that my big ass head was heavy as she tried her hardest to keep me up to pull my sweater off.

I woke up the next morning, I told Nia about my college roommate who was going to be in town for a week, and it was understood that I needed to be a good host as it was his first time in the city since we graduated from college. Nia was disappointed, but she understood my position. I was the luckiest man on earth because my roommate's visit to New York bought me a little more time. Nia wanted to have a quickie before I left, but I told her that I had to be at the airport in less than fifteen minutes to pick up my guest.

Chapter 35
Concealing My Fear and Pain

I picked up my old roommate, Kenny, from John F. Kennedy International Airport a couple of hours after I left Nia's house. I had lied to her about the time that I needed to pick up Kenny. He was full of life and I knew exactly what he was thinking. "What's up, dawg? You look good, man," Kenny said as we embraced brother style. "I've been good, man. What's up wit you?" "Man, ain't nothing up, but these white boys trying to drain the energy out of a brother at work." I knew soon that Kenny would ask me about the fine ass women at my club. He knew that I had been running the club for a while and he also knew that I always kept a stash of women like drug dealers keep a stash of dough. However, my stashing days were over and I was too worried about my health to even think about women. Kenny was my savior in one way with Nia, but he was also gonna be a pain in the ass for a whole week. My days of banging a slew of women night after night were over and I knew Kenny came to New York from D.C. on a scavenger hunt to get as much ass as he could.

I was watching at Kenny's exuberant energy for ass and I started reflecting on my life and thinking about the possibility of him falling victim to the "monster" like I might have. Back in college, Kenny and I were in constant competition with each other regarding women. If he brought a tall light-skinned woman back to the room with him one night, I had to go out and find an even taller and finer woman to top his woman and vice versa. We even did a ménage a cinq (five) once. It was the two of us and three women. That was the craziest shit we ever did. Kenny was on the basketball team at school, so it wasn't hard for him to get girls either. We were both good-looking athletes and there was an abundance of ass available to us.

We met these three chicks once at a party on campus and they were down for whatever. They were visiting from Long Island University. Kenny and I brought them back to our off-campus apartment to play strip poker and the next thing we knew, we were all standing butt naked in the middle of the living room. Two of the girls were pretty much confirmed, but we worried about the third leg. She was the most aggressive out of all three and she was the one that took charge and led the whole orgy. Our altered state of mind allowed us to be free without any conscience. An alcohol-induced state of mind can lead to a lot of dumb and stupid shit. I remember how Marjorie, the aggressive one of the bunch started attacking one of her girl's breasts then asked me to give her a hand with the other one. Before I knew it, I had two breasts in my face and two in my hands while Kenny was in the corner with some lips wrapped around his dick.

I couldn't let Kenny have all the fun. As I glanced over and noticed the effortless suction this girl applied to Kenny's dick, I wanted my own blowjob. Marjorie obliged and Lisa soon followed. Talk about a Doublemint commercial. I had the pleasure of double luscious lips wrapped around my ten-inch dick while I looked to the heavens. It was like Marjorie and Lisa were trying their hardest to prove to me that they could out-suck each other. Kenny soon joined us. We stood there like two black kings as the three white women from Long Island University sucked the hell out of us. I could

171

see the pleasure of handling two big black dicks on their faces. Sarah was the quietest of all three, but she was the freakiest. She had her pussy and tongue pierced and the sensation of her ring around the shaft of my dick was like nothing I experienced before. At one point the other two women stood back to cheer Sarah as she held each of our dicks in each hand and was sucking back and forth like the cameras were rolling. It was a little weird because I had known Kenny for two years and I had never seen him naked until that night and the same with him regarding me. Pussy can always take away all the discomfort of men.

As Sarah went on a sucking marathon, all Kenny and I could do was shake our heads at these crazy white chicks that were willing to get fucked in an orgy by two black dudes that they didn't know. Okay, I'm not gay or anything, but I needed to make sure that I wasn't getting outdone by Kenny. I had him beat by a good half of an inch in length and maybe half of a millimeter in thickness. The other two women who were obviously habitual dick suckers could tell that Sarah's mouth was starting to cramp on her, so they offered to take over for her. I opted for Lisa because I had already sampled Marjorie's skills, and Marjorie went to Kenny. The blowjob fest continued for another fifteen minutes until Sarah came back with her ass spread wide open and asked me to stick my dick in her asshole. I didn't know why she wanted me to fuck her in the ass, but the shit sounded exciting to me, so I rolled a condom down my dick and I entered Sarah's ass with ease. I had never even been in a pussy that was so easy to enter. While I fucked the shit out of Sarah's ass, Kenny was in the corner eating Lisa while Marjorie went up and down his dick taking it in her asshole, too.

When I noticed Kenny eating that white girl, all I could think about was "is that negro out of his damn mind?" We didn't even know these girls, and his mouth was buried deep inside this girl's pussy. I knew we were trying to outdo each other, but there was no way I was going to start eating some girls who let me fuck them in the ass the first night we met. Fuck that bullshit virgin shit that they believed. I could hear the girl moaning and shit like Kenny was taking her somewhere she had never been. He wasn't doing much with his dick though because Marjorie left him and came to me. I fucked the hell out of Marjorie's ass while I finger fucked Sarah. Sarah even started eating Marjorie's pussy while I fucked her in the ass. When I was about to cum, I wanted it to be like a porn flick. I cocked Sarah and Marjorie's heads back and splattered hot ice cream all over their faces. Kenny was in the corner screaming like a little bitch as he came while Lisa took his dick down her throat.

That night we received the blowjobs of our lives and we fucked the hell out of these three women's assholes. And that's all we fucked that night because they refused to allow us to fuck their pussies. We later found out it was common among some white women to get fucked in the ass because they wanted to save their pussies for their future husbands. It was their way of claiming virginity. Virgins my ass!

As I reflect on that night and many other nights where Kenny and I had many sexual romps with many women, I started to wonder whether some of these women had actually contracted HIV/AIDS over the years. It wasn't unusual for us to have as many as five or six casual sexual encounters with different women. Then I also wondered if Kenny always protected himself when he slept with these women. I knew that I had slipped a few times and that was basically because of poor judgment and lack of fear.

As I glanced over to see the enthusiasm in Kenny's voice when he started talking about his plans to get laid everyday while he was in New York, I knew he hadn't slowed down. Kenny and I were buddies, but I couldn't tell him that I was suffering from the fear of HIV. I tried to downplay the whole thing by telling him that I was engaged and that I had turned in my player membership card, which I did. Kenny wouldn't buy it. "Get the fuck outta here. You can't give up pussy just like that," he said to me. "Man, shit ain't the same way it was in college. I found the woman of my dreams and I'm looking forward to settling down with her." "Man, all this time you been in love, why you never said anything to a brother?" He asked. "Your ass ain't believing me now, why would you have believed me over the phone?" I said to him. "True dat! But look here, player, I'ma try to get my mack on while I'm out here and I would really appreciate your support. I ain't saying to dib and dab in any pussy or anything, but hang out with a player. I might need a wing man and you can talk the bitch to death until I bust my nut." Kenny was stupid like that and I knew he was seriously joking.

Like I said before, I didn't mind having Kenny as a guest at my house because it took me away from Nia at least until I confirmed whether or not I was HIV positive.

However, I knew that he was gonna start getting on my nerves soon with all his pussy chasing talk. This guy lived and breathed pussy. The fact that he was college educated, handsome and sometimes arrogant, made women cling to him. Kenny's presence made me realize as much as Black women complain about finding a good man, they always seem to overlook the great catches for the assholes. A person like Kenny had more than enough of his share of women on any given week. When I was out there being a dog, I was appreciated by most. Some of the women that I used to mess with before I got with Nia would get angry with me when they called and I told them I couldn't fuck them anymore because I had a girlfriend. Some even went as far as calling me soft. Women will always be a mystery to me, and motherfuckers like Bobby Brown will continue to have four, five kids by four, five different women and still find one that's stupid enough to think that she may be the one. At least Kenny wasn't having children with the women he was sleeping with. Well. At least that's what I thought because he never mentioned any kids to me.

Chapter 36
From Brother to Brother

"So Kenny, are you gonna continue to sleep around with women until your shit can't get hard anymore?" I asked. "Hell nah, man. When my shit can't get hard anymore, I'ma start using Viagra, baby. Shit with all these new drugs out now to help a motherfucker get an erection, a brother can be a player for life now," he answered. I could tell that Kenny believed that bullshit statement and I knew he wasn't done because he had more "science" to drop on the subject. "Look Ron, these old dudes are making it hard for a player out here and I'ma have to return the favor when I get older," he said. "What do you mean?" I asked. "Well, I'll put it like this. Back in the day, a young brother like me didn't have to worry about competition from these old geezers. There was no Viagra and these limped dick motherfuckers couldn't satisfy the women they were being sugar daddies to. They came to guys like me while these old cats paid their bills. Now, these old cats are having four-hour erections and putting it down old player style. Some of these women don't care how they cum as long as they're cumming. We're no competition for these dudes because most of them are more established financially and no longer have to pay for their mortgage or college tuition for their kids. So they spend most of their money on these young chicks." "Man, where the hell did you come up with that?" I asked. "Man, you ain't gotta believe me. Just look at the divorced rate for older couples. There's a bunch of lonely old women out there because of Viagra," he said.

As I listened to Kenny, I realized that he made a valid point. However, not every older man was running to the younger women because they suddenly could afford to buy a long lasting erection. Many of those bastards died as a result too, but what's a better way to go? As friends, Kenny and I never really had any serious discussion about family life. We both knew that we wanted to finish college and go on to do great things with our lives, but I wanted to hear Kenny's plan for the future. "So Kenny, are you ever gonna get married and have children?" I asked. "What are you talking about, man? I got like five kids already," he answered. "Man, when did you have all them kids?" I asked shockingly. "Shit, I had my first one when we were sophomores in college. All these bitches couldn't wait to get pregnant by me because they all thought I was gonna go pro. If I didn't blow my knee out, some of these bitches would be paid today, especially that ho named Juliet." It was obvious that Kenny still had no respect for women and even more so that he wasn't using a condom all the time either.

When he mentioned Juliet, all I remember was this innocent freshman girl that Kenny went out of his way to woo into sleeping with him. Juliet wasn't impressed with his basketball status on campus. She didn't even know he was a basketball player until he brought it up. She was a really nice girl and Kenny took her virginity. "If I remember correctly, Juliet left school after the fall semester, right?" "Yeah that ho left school because she claimed I got her pregnant. I knew I wasn't the only one that hit the skins. That bitch was trying to tell me that she was a virgin like I was gonna believe it," he said. "So why didn't you believe her?" I asked "Man look, every woman I met on that campus was a virgin until they started sucking my dick and showing their true skills. So how the fuck was I gonna believe that she was a virgin when most of these freshmen came in the school acting like virgins?" he retorted. I could only shake my head as Kenny started to unload his ignorance on me. "Man, you know that bitch had the nerve to call me to court for child support," he said. "Well, were you helping her out?" I asked. "Man, come on, how was I gonna help her out when I was still in school?" "What about the fact that she had to drop out of school because you got her pregnant?" "I didn't know that kid was mine and I still don't know. That blood test ain't always accurate. They say when a woman wants a guy badly that the kid can come out looking like the man she wants," he said. Kenny was just a tall glass of ignorance. I definitely knew that there was no way that I was going to entertain him for a week.

Back in college, Kenny and I didn't spend too much time getting to know each other because of my football schedule and his basketball schedule. However, he did mention on a couple of occasions that he had about twelve brothers and sisters that he knew of from his dad and that he saw his dad only three times during his whole life. I could see that the cycle hadn't been broken and Kenny was headed down the same path as his father. His education didn't mean shit because they don't teach you how to be a responsible parent in college. Kenny was still that ghetto boy who got lucky because of his athletic ability. He still needed guidance and a positive mentor in order for him to have been a responsible man. I thank God everyday for my parents, especially my dad for being around. There are so many brothers out there like Kenny who continue to repeat a cycle created by our fathers and forefathers and most of the time they don't have the good fortune to think about their bad situations in order to change it and make it better for their offspring.

I may not have planned to hang out with Kenny for a week, but he was gonna get a piece of my mind about his children. Not only that, he was possibly exposed to HIV and AIDS just like I was. I didn't want to be a hypocrite, but I needed to let Kenny know that he needed to take care of his responsibilities. "Look man, I think you need to start changing your attitude about your kids and your baby mamas. Back in college, you used to be angry with your dad because he was never around for you, but you want to do the same thing to your own children," I said to him. "Ron, you're not in my situation, so you can't know how I feel. I go to court almost every six months because these bitches want more money for child support. Every time I get a raise at work, I don't see it because it goes straight to one of these hos. I'm tired of living for them and having to take care of them and their boyfriends," he said angrily. "Ok, I see…that's how you feel about it. You think you're taking care of the mother instead of the child. First of all, you have no one to blame but yourself for having all these children with all these women. And second, children are expensive and they need a lot of shit. I'm sure none of your baby mamas are millionaires and if they could do it alone, I believe that they wouldn't bother you at all." "Man, are you sticking up for these bitches? You don't even know these hos. They some trifling hos trying to keep a man down for no reason," he screamed. "They were the same trifling hos that kept your dick hard and you weren't patient enough to put on a condom. Either way, your kids are your responsibilities and you need to own up to it, bro." "Now you're holier-than-thou? Fuck you, Ron. You did just as much dirt as I

179

did, but you don't see me judging you," he yelled at me. "Man, I'm not judging you. I'm telling you as black men we need to step up to the plate and own up to our responsibilities. We can't always let our dicks do the thinking for us and not pay the consequences. You said you have five kids, but ever since your plane landed, all you've been talking about is getting more pussy. That's that shit that got you in trouble to begin with." "You know what, man? You can drop me off at the Holiday Inn down on the right and I'll find my own way around New York," was the last thing Kenny said to me before exiting my car.

I understood that Kenny felt attacked by me, but he could only see things from his own perspective. He never stopped to see how things look so differently for the woman. I don't blame the men one hundred percent for the unplanned pregnancies and the bastard children that the women bear, but brothers have to start seeing their part in impregnating a woman. I've heard men say, "she knew I couldn't afford a kid, but she went and had one anyway," but they don't realize that sometimes it's not a choice. What pisses me off the most is when I see a young woman barely twenty-two hauling three or four kids by two or three different men and they want to blame the world for their situation. Yeah, those men are responsible for their part, but the women created that situation. It's as simple as "put on a condom or we ain't fucking." It couldn't be any more blunt than that. And most men will opt for the condom because pussy is just that important to them. I wish all the women who lay down with me without using a condom gave me that ultimatum. My mind would be so much more at ease right now.

I also realized that I couldn't be angry with Shauna when I saw her in the hospital. I played my part and I exposed myself by choosing to sleep with her unprotected. Those sixty minutes of pleasure could possibly turn into a lifetime of pain. Okay maybe I'm lying about sixty minutes. I still might have a lifetime of pain damn it!

Chapter 37
Still Waiting

Since I had planned to use Kenny's visit to stay away from Nia, I decided to keep that as an excuse even though I was never gonna see him again. Nia didn't have to know that we fell out. I contemplated talking to Myles about my possible ailment, but I knew he would open his big mouth to Chenille and my business would be all over New York City in no time. Even Shauna didn't bother telling Chenille about her condition because she knew that Chenille would judge her and start running her mouth. I decided to bury myself into my work until I got the results from the clinic.

I never realized how boring life could be without Nia. I was trying my best to keep busy at work, but I kept missing Nia and through force of habit, I would call her and stay on the phone with her for hours. She started to wonder if I was spending much time with Kenny. I couldn't be with Nia physically, but I wanted her near me on the phone. I had grown accustomed to being with her almost every day after work. I knew Nia was my soul mate because I felt like I lost part of myself without her. Sitting around and waiting for a test to confirm my life was taking a toll on me. While I stayed away from Nia, I tried my best to spend as much time with Shauna as possible at the hospital. I wanted to give her hope, maybe her spirit would have been lifted enough, and her desire to live would have strengthened.

Everyday after work I went to the hospital and sat by Shauna's bedside. I was looking at my fate everyday and I was not afraid. I was ready to deal with the consequences. My biggest issue was Nia. I felt she didn't deserve to pay for my mischievous behavior. I only hoped that my test would be negative. Sometimes I sat by Shauna's bed and wondered how could such a perfect beauty wither to nothing because of a simple disease. Is it really the end of the world? Men have always had a weakness for beautiful women and now more than before beautiful women are the deadliest things walking the earth. I reflected on all the other beautiful women that I slept with just because they were beautiful and I thought about my own prejudices and stereotypes. I always thought that people who cared enough to get a college education wouldn't be careless enough to catch such a disease. I should've looked in the mirror because I was the most careless educated person I knew.

I always thought that I could spot an HIV carrier by the way they looked or their lifestyle. As a young boy, I wasn't educated much about the disease and my parents didn't talk much to my brother and me about sex. As long as we didn't bring any babies home to them, they were happy. Now, I only wish that I brought a baby. At least I would not be worried about my life getting taken away from me. All the risks associated with HIV and AIDS weren't part of my life. I wasn't an intravenous drug user, I was not homosexual and I hadn't had a blood transfusion all my life. Come to find out through my research, those weren't the only risks, they were more like prejudices. Anybody who didn't take the precautious measures to protect themselves during sex is at risk. It is not a homosexual disease or a drug user's disease, it's a people disease and my ignorance kept me in the dark.

I also reflected on the many athletes and rap stars that Shauna could've possibly slept with unprotected. The domino effect of this disease from one person to the next was huge. Shauna alone had to be connected to at least ten to twenty people and if they each slept with an additional twenty that would soon grow to a big portion of the community and before we know it, everybody in this world would have known someone who died from AIDS during their lifetime on earth. The domino affect of this disease is huge. The six degrees of separation theory must've been considered when AIDS was being created. We're all separated from this disease through only one sexual encounter. Shauna was the first for me and she was my eye-opener. There is a big difference between talking about something and actually seeing it. If I had seen pictures of AIDS victims when I was in high school and college, I would have wrapped my dick in aluminum foil when I slept with a woman, forget condoms. AIDS is really scary and anybody who's never seen an AIDS patient cannot possibly understand the magnitude of the metamorphosis that this disease can cause.

This disease gave me time to reflect on the possibility that Shauna was leaving my life all together. Maybe I shouldn't have been so mean to her sometimes. She still wasn't humble because of the disease, she was humble because her life was being cut short and she didn't appreciate the people who cared about her when she had them in her life. The most physically beautiful woman I had ever seen finally showed some humility in the face of death and it was hard for me to absorb. Was I going to start changing as a person if I found out I was positive? I wondered.

One day while sitting by Shauna's bedside holding her hands, I could see her cracking a smile unexpectedly. "Ron, you know you are the nicest guy that I've ever known. I don't know why I had to mess things up between us. I knew you were driven. I also knew that you would make a good husband and father one day, but I wanted to be rebellious and I needed the attention of men. Not having my dad in my life caused me to make a lot stupid decisions and mistakes. In addition, I will always regret making the mistake of forcing you out of my life. You're a good guy and Nia's a lucky woman to have you," she said. "Well, I don't know how lucky she is to have me now. I might possibly end her life with this terminal illness," I said to her sarcastically. "You're one of the good ones and God always knows how to spare the good ones. I've been silently praying for you and I usually don't pray much, so that means I haven't asked God for much of anything. However, I did ask him to save you. People need you on earth and you can help change the lives and thoughts of others. Maybe you're experiencing this because you're a chosen crusader for change for this disease in the community," she said earnestly. I only smiled because I saw Shauna maturing right before my eyes.

Chapter 38
Facing My Fate

The fact that I owned a nightclub that generated a lot of money and was probably worth seven figures weighed heavily on my mind as well. In the event of my passing, I wanted my dad to gain part ownership of the place and I wanted to make sure that I was provided for and taken cared of in case my health started to deteriorate rapidly. I scheduled an appointment to go see an attorney about my last will and testament just in case. I felt it was important to do this because Nia had been an important part of the growth of my business and I needed to reward her for all her hard work. Since I wasn't going to be around to be a husband to her, she had to benefit in some way. I didn't want to leave it up to my family to decide if Nia was entitled to anything. I knew what she had done to help me with the club and I wanted to show my gratitude.

In my will, I left Nia with a ten percent interest of the club and the rest went to my parents and my brother. While I was alive, I had total control of everything, but in the event that I became incapacitated, my mother and father were to make all the decisions regarding my life. I still didn't want to tell my parents anything because I didn't want them to panic. I also informed my lawyer that he not to say anything to my family until my passing. He wondered why a person so young was writing a will, I told him that I wanted to be proactive. "It's funny because most Black people generally don't have wills because they don't think that they're ever dying. You're of the few Black folks that ever came to my office for a will, are you dying?" he asked. I almost wanted to tell him yes, but I didn't want to give this

White man the satisfaction of knowing too much about Black folks even though he was right. "No I'm not dying," I said defensively. "I think my statement offended you. I wasn't trying to be offensive. I just wanted to applaud you for coming in here to see that your business and family is taken cared of in case something happens to you. At least your assets won't be held in some estate by the state until they decide what to do with your money," he said. "I'm not offended and I understand what you mean. However, I need to tell you a little about my people as well. Most of us are not used to having so much money. We weren't even allowed to have bank accounts, not only that we weren't allowed to read for many years, so we couldn't handle a bank account anyway," I told him.

I continued, "as far as us not planning a will in case of our passing, I attribute that to Black people learning a great deal about being selfish while they were working the cotton fields. Just like any other cycle that continues to hinder our growth, it will take some time for us to let go of our selfish ways in order to strive, but we're working on it. I also don't want you to misinterpret what I meant by selfish. Our parents are selfish in a way that they don't trust that their children could handle their business as well as they can. Therefore, they hide their money and assets because they don't want to see it wasted while they're alive. Instead, they rather leave their kids to fight over their assets after they're dead and gone. I know it makes no sense, but it's all connected to slavery." I could tell that this white man didn't want to hear anything else from me. He simply had me sign the forms and told me he'd be in touch.

I also made provisions for my body to be cremated after my death. I've never been interested in having my body buried six feet under for the benefit of rodents, worms and other earthly creatures waiting below to devour some human flesh. The idea of having my body intact for an afterlife was ludicrous to me. How can anybody's body stay intact if the flesh is withered away after burial? I was comfortable with all my arrangements and was ready to deal with my fate.

I received a phone call from the counselor at the hospital early on Monday morning. Nothing much was said over the phone other than the fact that I needed to go in and sit down with the counselor to discuss my results. Part of me was anxious and the other part was afraid. It took me forever to shower and get dressed. I finally mustered the courage to drive down to the clinic to learn my fate. After arriving at the clinic, I was told to sit and wait in the lobby area because the counselor was busy telling some other fool about his/her last days on earth. How the hell you're gonna make me wait to find out if I have a deadly disease? That shit wasn't fair and I almost walked out. I could feel the affect of the result of the test in the pit of my stomach and it almost caused me to defecate right there in the hallway. I had to run to the bathroom before I shit on myself.

While sitting with my ass up in the air on that nasty ass toilet, I wondered how many people with AIDS sat on that same toilet and how that shit was gonna affect me even though I was in a squatting position avoiding all contact with the stool. I still didn't want to believe that I needed direct contact of exchanged bodily fluids in order to contract AIDS. As much as the counselor told me

188

about the ways that HIV could be transmitted, I still didn't believe a goddamn word she said, just like I didn't believe that I had long to live. Sitting on toilet would have sped up the process for the disease as far as I was concerned. I wanted to conserve time and the fear of death was starting to take over. As much as many of us claim that we're not afraid to die, we're scared out of our pants when we know we're gonna die. I wish that I had someone at the hospital with me that could hold my hand. Perhaps, I didn't give Nia as much credit as she deserved. Maybe she would've been my pillar of strength through this whole ordeal, I thought.

Then finally, after dropping about fifteen pounds of waste in the bathroom and stinking up the joint like a dumpsite, I was ready to go back out to find out the results. I would have left the toilet sooner, but a couple of people came in and made comments about my shit that would've embarrassed me. "It smells like somebody died in here," the first man said before running out of the bathroom. I held my feet up so he wouldn't be able to identify the culprit. "What the fuck is that? Do that stinking shit at home, not in a public bathroom," said the second man before running out to catch his breath in the hallway. Again, I had to hold my legs up to keep from exposing my feet in order to stay inconspicuous. I knew that my own habit was to bend down and look at the person's shoes in a bathroom in order to identify the nasty person taking a nasty public dump. I did not want to be identified and I didn't want anybody pointing any fingers at me.

I snuck out of the bathroom unnoticed, feeling like I just walked out of a Jenny Craig weight loss center. I was light on my feet as I dashed around the corner to avoid any onlookers. Just as I went to get a seat, the counselor came out screaming my name out for everyone to hear, "Ronald Murphy!" "Here," I answered in a low tone. "Sir, can you please follow me?" she asked. Her tone scared the shit out of me because I could sense her pity. I only needed pity if I was gonna die and this lady didn't crack a smile.

I have never been claustrophobic, but after entering this small little office, I started to feel like the walls were closing in on me. It was as if my feet were suspended in the air; I was upside down; and the room was spinning. She opened a folder with my name on it and I was trying my best to read her body language. "Mr. Murphy, I would like to tell you that your test is negative, but that does not mean that you've earned the right to go around sleeping with people without protecting yourself. There must've been a reason why you felt you needed to be tested. Also, you should probably continue to test yourself every six months if you've had unprotected sex with anybody during the last few months." I breathed a sigh of relief after she told me that my test was negative. I thanked and hoped that I would never have to see her again.

Chapter 39
Start Spreading the News

My next stop was at the hospital to see Shauna. She was the only person who could share in my excitement. No one else knew that I had been walking around with this cloud of fear over my head for weeks. I couldn't tell Nia because she probably would've wanted to kill me for possibly exposing her to this deadly disease. On my way to the hospital, I stopped at this flower shop in Brooklyn and I told the florist to put together two very special arrangements for me. One was for Shauna and the other was for Nia. I was skipping like a happy kid as I made my way through the halls of the hospital. My enthusiasm for life returned and now I had to continue to pray for Shauna. I knew there was no cure for the AIDS virus, but I wanted her to be around a little longer.

I couldn't wait to spread the good news about my negative HIV status to Shauna. God had answered her prayers and spared me. As I slowly approached the door to her room, I noticed the tag with her name had been removed. I wondered if she was transferred to another room. I went to the receptionist's desk to ask if Shauna had been removed. The receptionist asked if I was a relative or friend, I told her I was a close relative. They called her doctor to talk to me because he had gotten familiar with me at the hospital. I visited Shauna almost everyday and most of the staff at the hospital knew that she was special to me. I could sense the uneasy feeling that everyone was displaying in my presence and I started to worry. As I stood there waiting for the doctor, I wanted to wring my hand around the receptionist's neck to get the information out of her. I was getting impatient and I needed to know what happened to Shauna.

A few minutes later, the doctor appeared. He took me to his office and informed that Shauna had passed away at three o'clock that morning. Because she had found out about her HIV positive status so late and the fact that it had developed into full blown AIDS, there was not much that the hospital could do to save her. Shauna always knew that she was not careful enough with her life and she feared that she had contracted HIV, but was too afraid to find out. I broke out in tears when the doctor told me that Shauna's life ended abruptly. "I was just talking to her yesterday, Doc, how could that happen so quickly? I asked. "Her immune system started to deteriorate at a faster pace and we don't have the medication to slow it down just yet. I'm sorry about your loss," he said.

At first, I was too ashamed to let the world know that I could possibly be HIV positive. I was even willing to suffer in silence. However, I didn't want Shauna to die in vain. It was bad enough that some of the people closest to her didn't learn of her disease because of the shame associated with it, but I was gonna let the word out and she deserved to have all the people who cared about her at her funeral.

I called Myles at work to see if he and Chenille could meet me after work for dinner. He sounded worried, but I told him that I needed to see both of them in person to talk about something important. Even though Myles and I were roommates, we hardly saw each other. He was very busy with his job and I stayed away from the house as much as I could when I learned of the possibility that I might be HIV positive. I spent most f my time at the office and I slept on the sofa bed in the back of my office. That sofa bed used to be the ultimate banging bed for me, and even Shauna and I shared some great times on that sofa. Everything around me reminded me of her and I couldn't believe she disappeared from my life just like that.

I saw the way that Shauna died almost alone in the hospital and it upset me. The fear of being shunned by friends forced Shauna to keep her condition a secret even from her best friend. I didn't give a damn how Myles, Chenille, Nia and even my parents viewed me anymore. I didn't want to feel the shame that I felt while I was going through my ordeal. It was time for me to let the world know that AIDS is a human disease and not something to be hidden from friends, family and people in general.

Myles, Chenille and I met at this little restaurant in Manhattan on Seventh Avenue. When they saw me, the expressions on their faces indicated that they knew something was wrong. The waitress came around to take our drink orders and while glancing at the menu Myles asked, "Are you all right, man?" "Actually, I'm not. I've been going through a lot the last few months and something horrible happened to someone that was dear to us once upon a time." My statement puzzled both Myles and Chenille. "Who are you talking about?" They both asked. "Well, there's no simple or sensitive way to say this, but Shauna is dead," I said. Chenille almost jumped from across the table to slap me across my face. "Boy, stop playing with people. I would've been the first one to know if Shauna died," she said. "I'm afraid I'm not

playing. Shauna passed this morning in the hospital."
"Shauna's not in no hospital. I just spoke with her about
a month and a half ago and nothing was wrong with her
then," she said. "Actually Chenille, a month and a half
ago, Shauna was still alive and battling AIDS in the
hospital, but because of your judgmental character she
didn't want to tell you that she had AIDS," I said to her
with an attitude.

I could see their bodies shift away from me like I was
gonna cough up the virus right in their faces. Their body
language showed a lot of discomfort in my presence and
I could see Myles pulling his silverware away from mine
in a subtle way. I said nothing to them as they exposed
their prejudices towards me. It was their ignorance that
kept Shauna from revealing to them that she was sick.
"How long did she know that she had AIDS?" they both
asked. "She knew long enough to die from it. She only
found out when she went to the hospital for a routine
check-up for the flu," I answered. "Don't worry I'm not
gonna sneeze on you and infect you with it." I said to
them after they shifted their bodies again to back away
from me. I continued, "Besides, I already had myself
tested and I'm negative. I wanted to let you guys know
because at one point you and Shauna were best friends
and I found it sad that she died with just me and her mom
by her bedside at the hospital." I wasn't trying to attack
them, but Chenille had always considered herself better
than Shauna and she had influenced Myles to think the
same way about me because of my former lifestyle. If
she only knew that Myles had banged more chicks than
Ron Jeremy, the porno star, back when we were in
college, she'd probably jump off a bridge.

We finally ordered our food and within a few minutes, the waitress came back with our entrees. In the past, Myles and I would try to taste each other's foods to see which entrée is better so we could order it on our next visit. However, this time he probably felt that I was poisonous. He pulled his plates as far away from me as possible. I wanted to kick him in his nuts under the table and bitch slap Chenille when she mentioned that we shouldn't talk while we ate because she didn't want anybody to spit in her food by accident. I knew all that shit was directed at me and I was trying my hardest to stay calm and cool under pressure. "So, how often do you have to be tested to know for sure that you're negative?" Myles asked. "The doctor says I should get tested every six months for the next year because the virus may not show up for a while," I answered. "Were you sleeping with Shauna unprotected?" Chenille asked. "Are you sleeping with Myles unprotected?" I asked sarcastically. "Well, it's different. Myles and I are in a long-term relationship and I'm on the pill," she answered. "Let me see, last time I checked, the pill doesn't protect anyone from STD's, and being in a long-term relationship doesn't mean shit," I answered with an attitude. What I really wanted to say to her was "Look, you stuck up bitch, Myles fucked more women unprotected than Pastor T.D. Jakes baptized born again Christians, and if I were you, I'd take my black ass to the clinic and get tested right away." I even recalled that Shauna told me that she and Chenille once had a threesome with this guy back in college. If she kept that shit up, I'd embarrass her ass in front of Myles. It would hurt if she received a dose of her own medicine. Oh, how soon do we forget?

It could've been convenient amnesia on Chenille's part, but she was just as much at risk as I was. At least, I knew my status. That chick had no idea about hers. Shauna could've caught the HIV virus back in college for all we knew. I wanted the conversation to refocus back on Shauna. "Her funeral is this upcoming Saturday, I'm sure her mom would appreciate our presence," I said to her. "I don't know if I could and face her in her coffin. I should've been around for her when she was alive," said Chenille. "Well, you can pay your final respects and ask for her forgiveness. I think Myles should go as well because we all met at the same time and we were all cool within the group. Also, her mom is accepting donations of all kinds from the people who cared about her. There's always a way to make-up a wrong," I said to them.

I could sense that Myles and Chenille felt like they were being attacked. I was emotional at the time and I didn't give a damn how they felt about anything. I knew it wasn't their fault that they didn't visit Shauna at the hospital, but Chenille's condescending attitude played a big role in it.

After we ate, I told them about the funeral home where the wake was taking place as well as the church for the funeral the following day. I didn't even bother hugging Myles because I didn't want to put him in a compromising position. After I left them that night, I learned that no matter how close I think people are to me, there's always something that can make them become distant from me. It was a hard lesson learned. In my case, it was the fact that I dated someone who died of AIDS.

It's not as if telling Myles and Chenille wasn't uncomfortable enough. Now I had to also tell the woman that I had been sleeping with for the last couple of years that I was exposed to someone who died from AIDS. I wanted to proceed with caution. Yes, Nia said she loved me, but she wasn't my mama. Many conditions came with her love, such as: don't expose my ass to any deadly diseases or I'm gonna leave your ass. I still hadn't seen Nia in a while, I was missing her and I needed her. However, I wanted to be honest with her. What's the point of planning a life with someone if you can't be completely honest with her?

Telling Nia about my situation was the hardest thing that I ever had to do in my life for many reasons. First of all, she and I had been having unprotected sex for a while and I knew that she led a less risky lifestyle than I did. Second, I was afraid to lose her. However, I loved her so much that the only thing I could do was be honest. There was no other way.

Walking up the last flight of stairs to Nia's apartment seemed like eternity. My feet were heavy, my head was spinning, my stomach was turning like I was about to have the runs and my mind was running a mile a minute trying to carefully choose the right words to use to reveal my potent news to Nia. I even forgot that I had a key to her apartment. I knocked on the door once but I got no answer, then a second time and finally on the third and loudest knock she came to the door asking, "Who is it?" "It's me, baby," I answered. "Why didn't you use your key?" she asked. "You know what? I totally forgot I have the key," I said to her as my hand started to tremble with my grip tight around the dozen roses that I brought for her. Nia could sense that something was wrong with me almost instantly. I was staring at her because I missed her pretty smile, beautiful skin and her affectionate ways. She pulled me in for a hug and asked, "Are you all right, baby?" My mouth wanted to say yes, but my mind intervened and said no. "Is there something on your mind that you'd like to talk about?" she continued. I felt like a thief who had stolen some expensive jewels and was about to be caught for some odd reason. "As a matter of fact, there is something that I need to talk to you about," I said nervously. "Well first, why don't you take off your coat, hand me my flowers and make yourself comfortable?" she said to me. I wanted to calm my nerves, but I didn't know how. I was reacting to the thought of losing Nia. She was my world and I wanted a long, happy life with her. I handed her the flowers and my jacket as I took a seat in the living room area.

Nia had never seen me so nervous since we'd been together. She offered to make me some tea to calm my nerves. I didn't even feel comfortable in her house anymore. It was as if I was coming to clean out my locker at the end of a football season with no certainty of a contract extension with my team. In other words, I was shitting bricks! My whole demeanor was suspect, but Nia was sweet as honey and didn't seem like she was up to anything. Guilt is the worse feeling in the world. It can drive a man insane. I could understand then why some murderers sometimes confess to killing people. They can't live with the guilt. I was guilty of exposing Nia to a deadly virus and it was eating me from the inside out.

After Nia brought me a hot cup of lemon flavored tea, I asked her to sit next to me on the couch. "I have something very important that I need to talk you about," I said to her as I sipped my tea. "You know you can tell me anything, baby. I'm here for you, and always will be," she said, smiling. "Well, baby, what I'm about to tell you is either gonna make us or break us. It's not something that's easy for me to do. It's not the best thing, but in a way, it's also not the worse thing," I said to her. "Will you come with it already? Nothing is going to separate me from my baby," she said confidently. Shit, *I* even got some confidence from hearing her words. "Baby, I want our relationship to be based on truth and honesty and that's why it's so hard for me to keep this to myself. I want you to be in my life forever and I want us to grow old and wrinkle together," I said cautiously. "Me too, baby. Now, will you please tell me what it is that you have to tell me!" she yelled out.

Nia was starting to lose patience with me and I didn't want her to get angry before telling her my news. "Okay, here we go. Remember how me and Shauna used to date way back before I met you?" I wanted to make sure I put a lot of distance and time between my relationship with Shauna and my relationship with Nia. "Yes, I remember Shauna. Did you cheat on me with her?" she asked nonchalantly. It was that calm before the storm attitude where a woman wants to react, but she decides to wait to hear the whole story before hitting her man over the head with the biggest pan she can find. "No baby, I would never cheat on you. That's not what this is about," I said to her. "What is it about then?" she asked. "Baby, she's dead," I said with a sad face. "Is that what you had a problem telling me? You probably want to go to her funeral to pay your last respects…that's fine, baby. I wouldn't get mad if that's what you want to do," she said

199

while smiling at me. I tried clearing my throat before I said to her, "That's not all, baby." "There's more. What can it be this time?" she asked. "Well, baby. Shauna died of AIDS," I said to her while holding my hands over my face to protect myself from the wrath of her fury.

I never expected Nia to faint after I told her the news, but that's exactly what happened. She straight loss consciousness. I knew it was a difficult situation because of all the stigmas attached to AIDS. The harsh reality of public humiliation for those who suffer from the virus didn't make it any easier. I didn't know what to do to revive her. My dumb ass went in the kitchen, grabbed a pot of water, and threw it on her face. She came to, coughing and screaming. I was hoping that she had forgotten what I said to her before passing out, but it was only a wish. Discomfort kicked in and soon we were both sitting in silence away from each other. I wondered what Nia must've been thinking about me, about us and about the whole relationship. Love seemed to suddenly disappear from the house. Anger took over and it was unleashed with no holds barred. "I wanted to have your children one day, I wanted to walk down the aisle and marry you, I wanted to live a long healthy prosperous life with you, but now you've ruined all of that. You're a selfish bastard who never thought about my feelings and my health. If you knew that you had been sleeping around with a slut, you should've warned me and I would've had the option to protect myself when I slept with you. I want you out of my house and out of my life!" she said angrily as tears welled up in her eyes. I didn't even get a chance to say my piece. I understood where she was coming from, so I just stood there and took it all in. She threw my jacket at me while holding the door open as a stream of tears rolled down her cheeks. I knew she was gonna be hurt and the worst case scenario was that I might lose her. Whether or not I was prepared to lose her, I didn't know at the time. All I knew was that I had to leave her alone and give her time to calm down and think about our situation.

Chapter 40
What To Do Next

I left Nia's house feeling bewildered. Part of me wanted to give up on the relationship, but my heart wouldn't let me give up. She was, without a doubt, the greatest woman I had ever met since I came out of my mother's womb. My mother was the first, of course. I was angry that she didn't give me the chance to tell her that I got tested and my test was negative. At least, she would've gotten some relief. The stubborn side of me wanted to say "to hell with her!" but my heart was too much into it already. At the very least, I found solace in the fact that she did not take my ring off and throw it at me. To me, that meant it was not completely over yet, and I still had a chance. That drive home seemed longer than usual and I was not in the mood to speak with Myles. For all I knew, Myles probably had his belongings packed and ready to move out before he got infected by me. It was just as well because I wanted the freedom of living alone and he was starting to cramp my style with Chenille around the apartment all the time.

I got home that evening and didn't pay too much attention to my surroundings. I went straight to the bedroom to sob in my own way. I called my father to see if he could run things for me at the club for a few days while I tried to sort out my situation. I picked up the phone and called his number, and he picked up on the second ring. "Dad, how're you doing?" "Fine, son" he answered in his baritone. "How's mom?" "Your mother's fine. She went to the grocery store," he answered. "Dad, I'm not feeling well tonight, do you mind running things at the club for me? As a matter of fact it might be for a few days," I said to him in a depressing tone. "Son, don't think that I haven't noticed the change in you lately, because I have. I know that you been spending your nights sleeping in your office and your mind been everywhere but business. I didn't want to say anything because you're a grown man, but you're also my son and I need to make sure that you're okay." I wasn't sure if I wanted to talk to my dad about my personal life over the phone, but I definitely needed his support. "Dad, you're right. I'm going through some things right now and I been meaning to talk to you to get your opinion on what I should do, but I can't do it over the phone. I will try to talk to you tomorrow. Just know that I'm okay for now," I told him. "Okay son, if you say so. I'll be at the club tonight at nine to set up." We said our goodbyes before hanging up the phone.

I wanted to sleep away my problems as if they were a bad dream, but I knew that I would wake up the next day and they'd still be around. I sat in my room contemplating what my next move should be to save my relationship with Nia. Deep down inside, I felt like I was tainted goods. I knew Chenille's big mouth would have my business out there in no time and before long, everyone would think that I was HIV positive. There would be no more social life. Black people know how to twist a rumor better than a Midwestern twister. I needed to talk to someone about my problems, but it had to be someone nonjudgmental and someone that could give me sound advice. I could talk to my mother and father, but they didn't really understand HIV and AIDS. I caught my dad making ignorant statements after Magic Johnson announced he was HIV positive back in 1991. He sided with Charles Barkley and felt that Magic Johnson was a liability to the players when he came back from retirement to play. Even though my mother was a lot more enlightened and educated about the disease, she still had fears. I didn't want to go to them for advice. That only left me one choice, my brother.

Chapter 41
My Brother's Keeper

My brother and I were always close. He never knew this, but I looked up to him even though he was younger than I was. I admire his focus and determination. Breaking into the literary world was a battle in itself, but after witnessing the births of two books by him and a third one on the way, I couldn't be anything but proud of him. As a writer, my brother was also very open-minded and was well rounded as a person. He read extensively and knew what the hell was going on in Zimbabwe minutes after it happened, either online and through reading one of his favorite newspapers or books. I remember when the subject of AIDS was raised in our household; he was always the one trying to tell my parents the proper information about the disease. Because of his age, nobody listened to him. Being the youngest person in a household has its disadvantages. A young person's opinion is often not respected. My brother got spoiled like a prince, but he had no say in anything. My parents always came to me when they had questions about certain subjects. I never led on that my brother was the brighter one of the two us, but I personally knew it.

The weather was kind of chill, so I decided to meet with my brother at a place where I knew he would enjoy and be comfortable. Starbucks in lower Manhattan was just perfect. There, computer geeks, geniuses, readers as well as fake intellectuals and pick-up artists pack up the place. I knew this because I used to be one of those pick-up artists. Whenever I was in need of intellectual stimulation, I went and bought one of those intelligent books and took it to Starbucks with me so I could meet a brainy chick. Those brainiacs surprised me on a few occasions. Some of them were expert "brain givers".

Anyway, my brother showed up a few minutes after I arrived. He wondered why I wanted to meet with him at Starbucks of all places and the reason. I knew it was going to be a hard task revealing to any member of my family the fact that I had come into sexual contact with a person who died of AIDS, so I chose a public place. We opted for a corner table away from the crowd. I warned my brother to keep his voice low because I didn't want anybody in my business. "Is this some FBI classified shit we're about to discuss?" my brother, Ricky, asked. "No. Why?" "Because we're sitting here whispering like we're in the middle of a lesson in elementary school," he said sarcastically. "Man, look, what I'm about to tell you is top secret, top secret between me and you. I don't want you running to mom and dad with this," I said to him. "What is it, big bro? Did you get one of those girls pregnant and you don't want your girlfriend to find out?" he said in a smart tone. "You got jokes. Look, Ricky, this is serious. I called you here because I need your support. I ain't got time for your jokes right now. I'm dealing with a real situation and I need your help," I pleaded with him. "Okay, no more jokes. I'll just sit here and listen to what you have to say."

Before I got into my discussion with Ricky, I wanted to know if he wanted something to drink. He asked for a cappuccino and I opted for a mocha frappe. After getting the drinks, I came back to the table and found Ricky on his laptop checking his email. His laptop was like his American Express card, he never left home without it. My brother never ran out of ideas for books. He was

constantly writing and thinking about his next project. I
was even afraid that what I was about to reveal to him
was gonna end up in a book. After he quickly ran
through a few emails, he showed me a couple of them.
They were from some of his readers who were showering
him with praise for his work. I was very proud of him.
He didn't know this, but I used to go on Amazon.com
daily just to read the reviews on his books left by his
readers. My brother made it a point to separate himself
from everyone who was part of this new urban-lit surge.
After reading his books and a few other authors who had
been dubbed urban-lit writers, I knew that my brother
was more of a contemporary writer. He dealt with issues
that mattered to people in his books.

I was finally able to get Ricky's full attention after he
shut down his computer. "Ricky, I don't know any other
way to do this other than just coming out and say it.
Remember that fine girl that I used to go out with?"
"You're talking about the tall light-skinned chick, right?"
he said. "Right...that one. Well, she died of AIDS and I
told Nia about it and I think Nia is going to leave me
because she thinks I got AIDS too. I've been tested and
my test came out negative," I was rambling on, but my
brother got up from his seat and came around to give me
a hug. "Ron, everything will be all right," he said as he
hugged me. "I can imagine what you went through when
you found out about this. How long have you known
this?" he asked as he stepped away to get back to his
seat. We didn't want people to think that we were a gay
couple hugging endlessly. "It's been a while now. I'm
okay, but I'm worried about losing Nia," I said to him.
"Man, you need to be worried about yourself right now.
And I'm mad because you didn't even call me to tell me

the minute you found out about this. I would've been there for you. Brothers aren't supposed to keep deadly secrets from each other," he said angrily. "I didn't want anybody worrying about me or feeling sorry for me in case my results were positive. I definitely didn't want mom and dad to find out, because it would've killed them."

I could see where Ricky was coming from, but at the same time, I was too ashamed to let anyone in on my secret. "Ron, I'm not saying this to worry you anymore than you already are, but you're gonna need to get tested continuously every six months for the next couple of years to make certain that you are negative. Did you tell Myles about it?" he asked with this "I'ma kick your ass if I'm the last person to know" look on his face. "Ricky, I don't want you to get upset at me, but I did tell Myles and his attitude started to change towards me," I said to him. "Fuck him! You've got family, you don't need him. He was never a true friend to begin with if he's gonna be like that with you," he said angrily.

I was a little pissed at the fact that Myles threw away every single piece of silverware that he ever bought after he learned of my situation. His door was now kept locked to keep his room from getting tainted from my supposed disease. I could've easily gotten angry and confronted Myles and it would've resulted in a fistfight and he probably would've gotten his ass whipped, but I chose to let it go. Since the co-op was in my name, I knew he was gonna have to be the one to move out. I wasn't expecting any type of notice from him. I wanted him to be gone without saying anything to me. As the famous proverb says, "With friends like that who needs enemies?" All I needed was my brother; my parents always taught us to be there for each other. I could count on Ricky being there for me. However, I wanted him to know the real reason why I didn't tell him from the beginning.

"Ricky, it's not that I put Myles ahead of you, but I knew that if I told you that I had found out that Shauna had AIDS, you would've run to mom and dad because you'd be worried about me. I didn't want to get them involved and I didn't want to worry you. You better believe if I found out I was positive, I was gonna let your ass know from the hospital right after I got my results. I ain't dying alone. I'm letting people come in and grieve with me. Forget that, it ain't nice dying alone. I witnessed it firsthand." Ricky was laughing at me because he knew that I was gonna be all right. "I can't tell you how to live your life, but you got to be careful, bro. I'm not ready to lose my only brother. I want to watch my kids kick your kids' ass and if a stranger jumps in, I want to watch them kick the stranger's ass for jumping in," he said laughingly. My brother always had a great sense of humor and I needed that laugh.

Chapter 42
Getting My Woman Back

I didn't have the logical sense to go back to Nia to plead my case to her. I wanted to be "Mr. Macho Man" by telling myself that I didn't need her in my life. However, a nice reality-kick in the butt by my brother woke me right up. After telling Ricky the whole story, he was able to see where Nia was coming from and told me that I needed to prove to her that she was all that mattered to me. "How would you have reacted if Nia came to you and said her ex-boyfriend died of AIDS?" he asked hypothetically. I really didn't know what to say. "Did the cat catch your tongue? I thought so. Your black ass would be in jail right now for overreacting," he said, sarcastically. In a way, he was right and I knew from the beginning that Nia had every right to be angry with me, but getting her back was going to be a task in itself.

I wasn't seeking any romantic advice from my brother, but I got it anyway. My counselor, as I called him, informed me to write a very apologetic letter to Nia to explain my situation and to make her understand that I was not out to hurt her. He suggested staying away from her was the best thing that I could do at the time.

After leaving my brother, I anxiously rushed home to get started on this beautiful letter that I wanted to write. A long hug from my brother before departing comforted a little part of my soul, and I knew that getting Nia back in my life was essential. When I got home, I kicked off my shoes and went straight to my desk to get started on the letter. I didn't even notice until the next day, the note that Myles left taped to his bedroom door, telling me that he

210

had moved out. I felt like it was my last ray of hope and I wanted to write the letter to my best ability. However, I wasn't much of a writer and I struggled a lot with it. I must've gone through a whole notepad. Each sentence that I wrote down seemed totally wrong. I didn't know how to express myself. I picked up the phone and called Ricky since he was the writer in the family.

"Yo Ricky! I'm having a hard time starting this letter. I went through a whole notepad and nothing I wrote down sounds right," I said to him after he picked up the phone on the second ring. "Ron, one of the first rules of writing is that it can't be forced. It has to come to you. Only your natural thoughts can flow on paper. You're an intelligent man with a college degree, so I know you know how to express yourself. Stop forcing it and let it come to you," he said to me. "Man, I can't even get started. I don't know what to say to her," I told him. "Your problem is that you're trying to write this letter with your mind instead of your heart. You're worried so much about losing Nia; you've totally blocked your heart out. You need to drink a glass of wine, relax and allow your heart to do the talking," he told me. Maybe Ricky was right. I was stressing the fact that I might lose Nia too much.

I decided to take his advice after hanging up the phone. I went to the bathroom and filled up the tub with warm water and some bubble bath. I took a glass of wine, a notepad and a pen to the bathroom with me. As I sat in the tub reminiscing about the special moments in our relationship, everything started pouring from my heart:

Dear Nia,

I want to start this letter by telling you how sorry I am for jeopardizing our relationship by foolishly exposing myself to the world without thinking that I would some day meet my special queen. I call you my queen because I plan on having a princess with you in the near future.

Anyway, I'm fighting hard to find the right words to explain the whole situation to you. First, I want you to know that I would never, ever, knowingly risk exposing you to any kind of illness that would take you away from me. The situation with Shauna happened and there's nothing that I can do about it, but I want to do something about us. I honestly feel that you are the best thing that's ever happened to me and I can't afford to lose you out of my life.

During the time we've been together, I've grown so much as a man and a person. The things that I yearned for before I met you are no longer significant to me. Now I look forward to your beautiful smile that brightens my day. I look forward to your sweet voice that gives me a sense of security. I look forward to your support that gives me the strength to face this cruel world everyday. I look forward to your words of encouragement that help to overcome the obstacles that I face in my life. I look forward to your patience that gives me motivation to strive. I look forward to your beautiful body and mind that stimulates both my northern and southern heads. I was just trying to be funny in a serious way with the last one. What I really want to say is that I miss you, baby, and I don't want to ever be apart from you again.

I've also written you a special poem that I hope you know came from the bottom of my heart.

It Could Only be You

As much as I love you, you're making me suffer
Without you I haven't a life, please don't make it any
rougher

Don't make it worse than it has to be
Show me that you want to be with me

A little tenderness will keep me holding on
I would hate to wake up tomorrow to find out you're gone

It Could Only Be You

You're the sunshine of my day and the moon of my night
My heart has a lot to say, some feelings I just can't fight

I very well know I've caused you pain, but you must
forgive me
It's tearing me apart knowing that you might leave me

If you look deep into my eyes, you can feel my pain

Falling in love again will never be the same.

It Could Only Be You

It's you who showed me what living life is all about
It's you who taught me love without a doubt

When I think about the good old days, I just break down
and cry
Now I go to sleep all alone at night and wonder why

I will always love you with all my heart
You can walk away from me, but you can't take away that
part.

I hope this letter finds you in peace.

Love always,

Ron

I wasn't accustomed to begging, I simply wanted to let her know how I felt. It was now up to her whether or not she wanted to give me a second chance. I took the letter and poem and transferred them onto sexy stationery before sending it over to her house the next day with a dozen stems of roses.

Chapter 43
Hoping For the Best

I did what I needed to do in terms of an attempted reconciliation with Nia. All I could do at the time was wait for her to get back to me. As I waited a couple of days after the flower shop confirmed that she had received my roses and letter, I started to panic. I started feeling that Nia was slipping through my hands. She had had enough of me and she didn't want to go through the heartache anymore, I thought. Calling her was definitely not an option. I was a grown man and I didn't want to run to my mama for comfort, but I had to. Mama knew best.

I really didn't want to divulge my business to my mom when I picked up the phone to call her. I wanted to talk to her in person. "Hi mama," I said through the receiver after she picked up the phone. Almost instantly, I felt like a little boy as her soothing voice brought comfort to me like a child waiting for a blanket. "Are you okay, baby?" she said with a concerned tone. "Yes, I'm all right. I need to talk to you about something important, mama. I know I haven't come to you for advice in a long time, but I need you for this one." "I'm always here for you, son. And before you say anything, your brother already explained to me what happened," she said. That big mouth! I thought I made it clear to him that I didn't want my mother and father to find out about my situation. "You know I've been praying for you ever since he told me. I know the Lord is gonna save my child from this deadly disease. You need to come back to the church, baby," she said before I could get a word out. I wanted to kill my brother at that moment for betraying my trust.

216

While my mother was on the phone with me, I was plotting to kick my brother's ass. That little rat bastard!

"You know your brother told me not to say a word to you, but I can't sit by and watch my baby get sick with some disease that only the Lord can cure," she said. "Mama, I'm not dying and I don't have any disease. I've been tested already and I'm not positive," I told her. "I know, baby, but that hoochie ex-girlfriend of yours is dead, isn't she?" she asked. "Yes, mama, and she was not a hoochie. She was a wonderful person in her own way," I answered. "Well, she's dead because she never went to church and prayed to ask God to take the disease away. I've been praying for you and your daddy, too. I can't wait for you guys to give up that nightclub business. It's a sin. But God is gonna spare my child cause I pray hard and good," she said. My mother was always overly religious. She was only able to drag the family to church on special occasions like Easter and Christmas. My dad didn't like her pastor too much. He was always asking the congregation for donations to fix something that was broken in the church. He must've asked for donations to fix the heating unit at least fifty times. Ever since I was a boy, there was always something wrong with the heat at the church every year. And every year the congregation donated money for a new system. In the summer, the air conditioning system was always broken, according to him.

"Is that nice girl you brought here still with you?" she asked. "She's not just any girl, mom, she's my fiancée. She's not with me right now, but I'm trying to win her back." "I hope you do, son, because ain't too many women gonna wanna be with a man who came into contact with a woman who died of AIDS," she said matter-of-factly to me. I was shocked at my mother's statement. Then again, I could really see where Nia was coming from. "Look, you're my son and I need to be as honest as possible with you when it comes to women. That poor girl is probably scared to death after you revealed your situation to her. She's not gonna just jump into your arms after that devastating news. You're gonna have to prove to her that you always have her best interests at heart. If I were you, I'd get some kneepads because you're gonna be doing a lot of begging for the next few months. Oh, also, keep a side budget for flowers, jewelry and other gifts she might like. This is huge," she said while laughing. My mother was always a joker when she needed to be.

My mother may have been joking, but I knew that she was right. Although Nia didn't strike me as the material type, I wanted to show her that I would go all out to get her back. I thanked my mother for her encouraging words and told her I loved her. "I'll be praying for both of you, because I don't want to be too old before I start getting some grandchildren. Your daddy is already getting on my nerves as it is. You're gonna have to give me something to occupy my time after I retire," was the last thing she said to me.

After talking to my mother, I knew I needed to step up my game in order to win Nia back. First, I had to settle a score with a little squealer. I placed a called to my brother while I was on my way to the restaurant to pick up some food. When he picked up the phone, it was as if my mother had just called him to tell him that she and I had just talked. Before I could even say anything to him, he jumped in, "Look Ron, I know you told me not to tell mom and dad about your situation, but I couldn't live with myself if something happened to you a few months down the line and they didn't know. Just because you took this test that came back negative, it doesn't mean that everything is all right with you. What if it comes back positive six months down the line? With this disease, you never know and I'm hoping it will be negative because I don't want to lose my brother, but in case you don't get the result you want six months from now, I needed to let them know. I want the whole family to support you, not just me. I can't afford to lose my only brother and together the family would try to do everything we can to extend your life if that's what has to be done. Before you say anything, I told dad as well." I guess I never saw it that way and my brother made a valid point. I did tell him that Shauna almost died alone in the hospital with the exception of me and her mother as visitors. "Ricky, I ain't mad at you, bro, because I can see where you're coming from, but next time I ask you to keep a secret, you better keep it or we're gonna be wearing our boxing gloves in the backyard to settle things the way we did when we were kids," I told him. "You sure want to go there? I remember stinging your ass a couple of times," he said jokingly. "But I always won. And what?" I said arrogantly. "I let you win because I didn't want my older brother to look bad in front of mom and dad," he said before quickly hanging up the phone.

My brother and I had that kind of relationship. He always wanted to have the last word and most of the time I let him because that was all I could do. It was all in good gesture. I love my little bro. The next time I saw my father, he gave me a big hug. Ricky had taken his time explaining the whole HIV/AIDS thing to my parents to lessen their fear. He had a way with words and for some reason my dad had nothing ignorant to say about HIV/AIDS anymore. My mother still believed that God was the only cure for the disease, though.

A few more days went by and I still didn't hear from Nia. I sent her flowers almost everyday with little notes telling her how much I love and missed her. She never responded. I know the poem thing is corny to some people, but that was my only hope. I started writing more poetry and emailing them to her every week. I was hoping that the next poem I sent to her would spark a reaction and it did. It was called "Just Thinking of You."

Just Thinking of You

I can just imagine you and I on an island somewhere very
far
Holding you in my arms under the stars.
Watch, as you walk away from me and hug you as you
walk towards me
We would be inseparable like flesh and bone
For without each other, we could not go on
There would be no argument, simply joy
Like the pubescent years, you'd be my girl and I'd be your
boy

220

You are so very sweet
You're my honey bun and my chocolate treat.

After reading my poem, Nia immediately called me. I was so giddy I didn't know what to do with myself. "Do you really mean those words in your poems?" she asked. "Of course, baby. You're the only person who could've brought those words out of me. I never in my life wrote poetry before," I told her. "I'm a little busy right now, but I wanted to call you to let you know that I appreciate all your efforts. I also want to say that I need a little more time to deal with the situation and I would love to have dinner with you on Friday on my roof top so we can talk," she said in her sweet tone. I was ecstatic. "Sure, baby. Take all the time you need. We'll talk soon and I'll see you Friday... Did you have a time in mind?" I asked. "Show up at eight o'clock sharp," she told me. "I will be there." Those were my last words to her before I jumped in the shower singing for joy. At least, I had my foot in the door. Nia was willing to give me a second chance. However, I didn't want to stop doing what I was doing to woo her back. I continued with the flowers and I read more Shakespeare and Maya Angelou poetry books than I care to mention in order to strengthen my poetry skills.

Chapter 44
Goodbye

Meanwhile, I still had a funeral to attend. Shauna's wake was also on Friday and I was there early because I wanted to help her mother with the set-up and everything else. I also brought a five-thousand-dollar check to help cover the funeral cost. I knew that her family was short on funds and I wanted to show my gratitude to Shauna. The funeral was in Brooklyn because she couldn't find an affordable funeral home in Manhattan. I was one of the first few people to arrive there. Her mother and a couple of cousins were there before me. After arranging the place to their liking, it was time to open the casket so people can view the body. Shauna had this somber look on her face. It was like God had forgiven her for all she'd done and she was on her way to heaven. Her mother applied her make-up and she tried her best to make Shauna look as beautiful as she could, but I could tell the difference. AIDS doesn't leave anybody beautiful.

I fought back tears as I stood by the casket to look at Shauna and reminisced about the time I'd known her. We had a lot of fun and she would surely be missed. I was laughing at the fact that even in death she affected my life. In retrospect, I believed Shauna was the first woman that I ever had deep feelings for since I started dating. I enjoyed her beauty, her smile and her personality, most of the time. She was also an intelligent woman who didn't always make the right decisions and choices in her life. Shauna's zeal to succeed in life far exceeded her ability to use common sense, sometimes.

The black sequins dress draped over her body, as she lay peacefully in her casket with her hands across her chest was about the only thing that I knew she would've hated. Shauna was classier than that; at least she wanted to be. Her mother's effort was good enough I guess. I just couldn't believe how quickly her life ended. We were still young and with the potential to be part of this great country's future. However, what I believed to be this man-created disease somehow came into play and started destroying the lives of people across the world.

As a slew of people made their way into the funeral parlor a few minutes later, I could tell who showed up to see what an AIDS victim would look like dead. The minute after viewing the body, they were ghost. Family members took over the two front row seats as I sat back quietly in the back observing the whole situation. There were fake condolences from people who claimed to have missed her, most of whom I had never met or seen when Shauna was alive. Her mother had quiet strength as she sat there watching all these fake family members who never as much showed up to see her daughter before she died. Shauna apparently had a lot of family and friends in death. I couldn't believe how people call themselves kinfolks, but they only get together during funerals and weddings. It took away from the notion of family. I decided to make an early exit because I could not stomach the scene. I gave Shauna's mom a long hug before leaving.

Chapter 45
Sadness to Happiness

Immediately after I left Shauna's funeral, I went straight to Nia's to have dinner with her. My whole attitude was optimistic and that part of me that was sad when I was at the funeral home completely left my state of mind. It was as if I was bipolar. My energy was at an all-time high as I anticipated a reconnection with Nia. While I felt bad about the death of Shauna, I didn't want to lose an important piece to my life. Nia was my future and I needed to make sure she was back in my life. For the past couple of years, I realized there are many available women out there, but many of them are not ready to become a wife, friend, partner, mother, companion and lover. Half the women that I've met in my past were looking for something they weren't even able to provide. I felt like I was coming to the table with everything. I mean I had the silverware, the tablecloth, the napkin and the meal, while they were just showing up to eat. That was what set Nia apart from the rest. Nia didn't ask of me something she couldn't provide for herself. She was there through my growth and I also watched her grow. She helped create the better man that I've become and it was only fair that she reaped the fruits of her labor. Nia encompassed everything that I ever wanted in a woman. She was ready for me and I was ready for her.

I arrived at Nia's place at eight o'clock sharp. I had to make a quick stop at this high-end liquor store in Brooklyn to buy a bottle of wine. I also stopped at Walgreen's to get a greeting card. I wanted to make sure that all bases were covered. After knocking on the door, Nia opened the door wearing a V-neck dress with three-quarter poet sleeves, fit shape that tied in the back. I had been longing to see those curves again and she looked sexy. I handed her the bottle of wine then gave her a hug, which seemed a little distant compared to hugs in our past but was warm. She led me to the rooftop where she had dinner ready by candlelight. I could tell that Nia had put a lot of effort into dinner and I had an empty stomach that couldn't wait to show appreciation for her cooking. As she looked me over in my black suit, black tie and my great smelling Armani Code cologne, she smiled. A smile that signified we were on the path to forgiveness.

I marveled in the moment. She could see the smirk on my face. I sat across from her, hopeful that she would give our relationship another chance. After pouring wine into her glass, I thanked her for giving us another chance. "You're not gonna just walk back into my life that easily, Mister," she said playfully. "I plan on working hard to get back in your good graces, Ma'am," I responded. I poured myself a drink then took a seat. Nia got up and served the salad first. She had Ranch dressing, as she knew it was my favorite. "I really enjoyed your letters and poems," she said as she placed a spoonful of salad on my plate. "The joy was all mine. You know I can't live without my baby." She smiled. It was silent for a few minutes as we both dug into our plates to enjoy the fresh salad that Nia had put together. The only sound that could be heard was the low munching and crunching of the lettuce and tomato in our mouths.

As I chewed my food, I couldn't stop admiring and thinking about all the good things that Nia had brought to my life. Even her imperfections were perfect to me. I knew she was the woman that I wanted to spend the rest of my life with and she needed to know how serious I was. In between bites, I said to her, "You know you don't have a choice but to let me back in your life. I won't take no for an answer." She wanted to smile, but she stopped in her tracks to ask me, "Did you ever sleep with Shauna while we've been together?" That question needed a quick response, but I couldn't be honest with her. I was already in the doghouse, and if I told her the truth, I would've lost her for certain. "No, I was never with Shauna while I was with you," I said with a straight face. I was only with Shauna once and Nia didn't have to know that. It was a stupid mistake and I felt it was something that I could take to my grave. "Are you sure? Your mouth says one thing, but your eyes say something completely different," she said. I felt like I was the hot seat for a moment. I had to regain my composure in order to appear sincere and believable. I honestly didn't want to lie to Nia, but I had no choice. I didn't want to lose the only woman that I ever felt so strongly about.

I looked straight into Nia's eyes and told her, "Can we please not talk about Shauna anymore. I would rather focus on my future wife." "Your future wife? I'm not sure if we're gonna be married any time soon. We're gonna have to wait and see how your test results come back for the next year or so," she said. I was taken aback by her comment a little, but she had every right to say what she said. The killer for me was the fact that Nia probably wasn't going to sleep with me until I was completely in the clear with my HIV status. It was something that we needed to discuss, but I put it on the backburner because I didn't want her to think that I only wanted her for sex. Her safety was also very important to me and I didn't want to risk it or screw it up altogether.

Nia and I pretty much sat there and enjoyed each other's company. It felt like we were getting to know each other all over again and it was okay. I often heard the proverb "Good things are worth waiting for," but I never understood the true meaning behind that proverb before my situation with Nia. Her face was still filled with glee at the sight of me, and that's what kept my heart beating for Nia. She had every reason to end the relationship, but she realized what we had, was important enough and deserved a second chance. As she sat across the table staring into my smiling face, she asked, "Are you ready for the main course?" "My stomach has been yearning for your cooking, you just don't know," I said. "Well, I'm glad that you didn't just miss me, but you missed everything about me," she said. "Of course, you're one in a million and very few people get to be as happy as I am," I confirmed.

While Nia was looking very sexy and tantalizing in her dress, I had no sexual urge whatsoever. All of a sudden, I found myself digging Nia, the complete person. It was love on a completely different level. The mere fact that she was even willing to see my face again said a lot about her character. Most women in Nia's position would have their brothers and cousins waiting for me with bat in hand for a beatdown, but I had found a woman with the kind of heart I didn't know existed. I started to develop a whole newfound respect for Nia. Her heart was truly kind and I felt like the luckiest person in the world. By the time she served the entrée, my mind had drifted somewhere and Nia and I were living in a nice upscale neighborhood with two children, a dog with the white picket fence. The aroma of her food brought me back to reality and I could see how I was going to make everything I just daydreamed about a reality.

"I made your favorites: chicken, macaroni and cheese, rice and peas with gravy," she said. I could feel my nostrils expand as I took a whiff of her great smelling food. Her motherly nature and her nurturing ways were reminiscent of my own mother, a character that is hard to find in an ever-growing world of self-proclaimed overly independent women who are looking for equality at all cost, and end up destroying the fiber of the family unit. After serving the food, she sat across from me and we began to eat. The food tasted even better than it smelled. "I miss you very much, you know," I said in between bites. "I miss you too, but I was also angry with you. I'm over it now, but I want you to know that as much as I love you, I'm not willing to die for you because of stupidity," she said. I really didn't know what to say, but I wanted to say something to show her that I appreciated her as a person and I was grateful to have her back in my life. "Baby, I will never jeopardize us this way again. I've made some foolish decisions because I didn't know any better. But now, I know what's important to me and I don't want to lose you." I could tell that Nia was amused by my honesty. "I hope you know that the only reason that you're here right now is because I share the same sentiments as you. I want a man who's gonna be a good father, great provider and puts his family first. I already know that you possess all those qualities. However, if you ever try to hurt me again, I'll cut you. I'm a Brooklyn girl, you know," she said affectionately.

It appeared as if I was out of the doghouse, but I still didn't want to rush things back to normal. I understood that she still had fears in the back of her mind and I wanted to make her feel at ease around me. After dinner, we sat on the couch cuddling while watching our favorite movie, *Love Jones*. Nia's body never felt so good next to mine. The simplest touch of her hand was satisfaction enough for me to create an emotional orgasm that felt better than any physical pleasure that I ever had in my life. I can't deny that I got an erection as I spooned her body on the couch, but the connection was all mental. That evening I realized that Nia deserved my unconditional love and respect and I vowed that I would do everything in my power to treat her like a queen for the rest of my life. The gods or the angels must've been watching out for me because I found an angel of my own way before I made it to heaven. In essence, my life was heaven on earth.

Chapter 46
Moving On

I thought about being the bigger man by placing a call to Myles to see if there was any way to mend our friendship, but Nia made me realize that I never did anything wrong to Myles. He was driven by his ignorance and our friendship suffered as a result. Most of us feel that a college education is supposed to broaden our minds and enlighten our spirits, but that's not always the case. The measure of a man is by his actions and to me Myles, even though I missed him, was not the man that I once called my best friend. Whether his decision to end our friendship and walk out of my life altogether was influenced by Chenille, I didn't want to know. It was us who made the decision to become best friends, so Chenille should not have had any influence whatsoever on the fate of our relationship. I felt dumped by him and a little part of me resented her. I also learned through my experience that prejudice could rip apart the heart of a good person without knowing the power of it.

Most of us walk around with preconceived notions of people, diseases and situations without realizing how they affect us as people. In every situation, I believe there's a lesson to be learned. Shauna's unfortunate demise to this disease taught me to reevaluate myself as a person, and my values as an individual. I did not want to walk around feeling any kind of way towards anybody on this earth again. I wanted to see people simply for who they are and allow *them* to tear themselves down from my perfect vision of them. Nia was brought into my life for a purpose and a reason. I wanted to use that to make my world better as well as everyone around me. My parents' view also changed and it made them better as people.

A little over a year had gone by before Nia and I got physical again. My quarterly HIV tests came back negative each time and I prayed to God everyday for giving my life a second chance. With my second chance in life, I also decided to volunteer my time as a support counselor at the local HIV/AIDS clinic in Brooklyn. I wanted help those people who felt hopeless, I wanted them to know that it was okay, and that the whole world didn't have their backs turned on them. My time at the clinic was something that I wish I had done prior to my personal experience with this deadly disease. So many of the people I met felt so isolated, and I believe the sadness that they had to deal with accelerated their death.

I also anticipated a call from Myles everyday for the last year or so, but it never came. I decided to close that chapter in my life and moved on. Nia and I got married. My brother was my best man and my whole family welcomed her warmly. We are now expecting our first child who's a girl, our very own little angel.

Motherhood and the trials of loving too hard and not
enough frame this story...The realism of these characters

will bring tears to your spirit as you discover the hero in
the villain you never saw coming...
Neglected Souls is gritty, hardcore and heart wrenching.
In Stores!!

Jimmy and Nina continue to feel a void in their lives
because they haven't a clue about their genealogical
make-up. Jimmy falls victims to a life threatening illness
and only the right organ donor can save his life. Will the
donor be the bridge to reconnect Jimmy and Nina to their

biological family? Will Nina be the strength for her brother in his time of need? Will they ever find out what really happened to their mother?

In Stores!!!

Betrayal, lust, lies, murder, deception, sex and tainted love frame this story... Julian Stevens lacks the ambition and freak ability that Miko looks for in a man, but she married him despite his flaws to spite an ex-boyfriend. When Miko least expects it, the old boyfriend shows up and ready to sweep her off her feet again. Suddenly the grass grows greener on the other side, but Miko is not an easily satisfied woman. She wants to have her cake and eat it too. While Miko's doing her own thing, Julian is determined to become everything Miko ever wanted in a man and more, but will he go to extreme lengths to prove he's worthy of Miko's love? Julian Stevens soon finds out that he's capable of being more than he could ever imagine as he embarks on a journey that will change his life forever.

The police in New York and other major cities around the country are increasingly victimizing black men. The violence has escalated to deadly force, most of the time without justification. In this controversial book, noted author Richard Jeanty, tackles the problem of police brutality and

235

the unfair treatment of Black men at the hands of police in New York City and the rest of the country. The conflict between the Police and Black men will continue on a downward spiral until the mayors of every city hold accountable the abusive members of their police force.

In Stores!!!

Just when Darren thinks his relationship with Tina is flourishing, there is yet another hurdle on the road hindering their bliss. Tina saw a therapist for months to deal with her sexual addiction, but now Darren is wondering if she was ever treated completely. Darren has not been taking care of home and Tina's frustrated and agrees to a break-up with Darren. Will Darren lose Tina for good? Will Tina ever realize that Darren is the best man for her?

In Stores!!

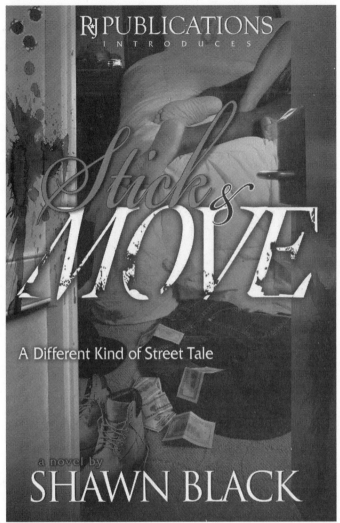

RJ PUBLICATIONS
INTRODUCES

Stick & MOVE

A Different Kind of Street Tale

a novel by
SHAWN BLACK

Yasmina witnessed the brutal murder of her parents at a young age at the hand of a drug dealer. This event stained her mind and upbringing as a result. Will Yamina's life come full circle with her past? Find out as Yasmina's crew, The Platinum Chicks, set out to make a name for themselves on the street.

In Stores!!!

237

Tina develops an insatiable sexual appetite very early in
life. Sheonly loves her boyfriend, Darren, but he's too far
away in college to satisfy her sexual needs.
Tina decides to get buck wild away in college
Will her sexual trysts jeopardize the lives of the men in
her life?

In Stores!!!

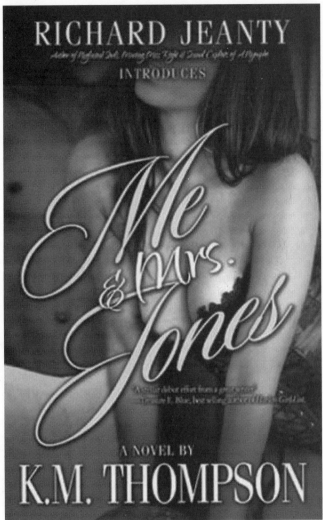

Faith Jones, a woman in her mid-thirties, has given up on ever finding love again until she met her son's best friend, Darius. Faith Jones is walking a thin line of betrayal against her son for the love of Darius. Will Faith allow her emotions to outweigh her common sense?

In Stores!!!

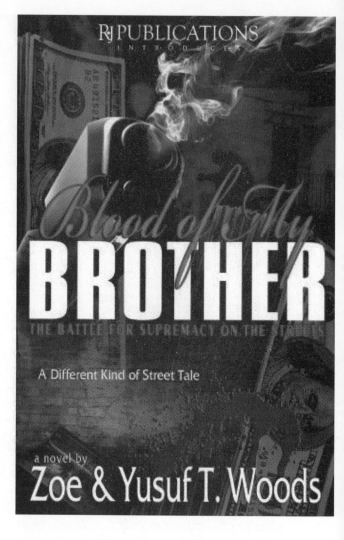

Roc was the man on the streets of Philadelphia, until his younger brother decided it was time to become his own man by wreaking havoc on Roc's crew without any regards for the blood relation they share. Drug, murder, mayhem and the pursuit of happiness can lead to deadly consequences. This story can only be told by a person who has lived it.

In Stores!!!

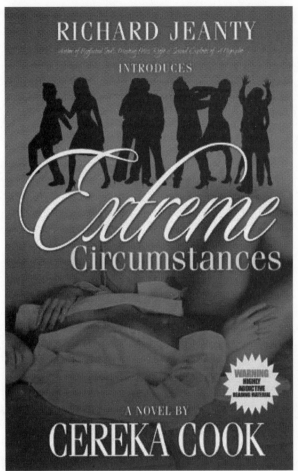

What happens when a devoted woman is betrayed? Come take a ride with Chanel as she takes her boyfriend, Donnell, to circumstances beyond belief after he betrays her trust with his endless infidelities. How long can Chanel's friend, Janai, use her looks to get what she wants from men before it catches up to her? Find out as Janai's gold-digging ways catch up with and she has to face the consequences of her extreme actions.

In Stores!!!

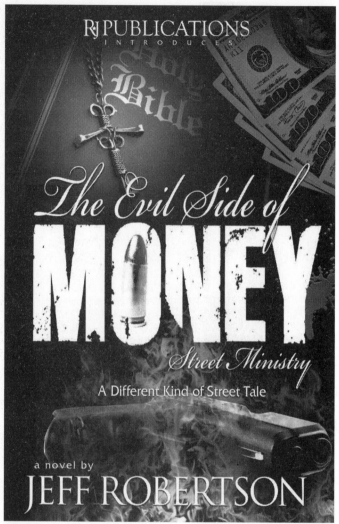

Violence, Intimidation and carnage are the order as Nathan and his brother set out to build the most powerful drug empires in Chicago. However, when God comes knocking, Nathan's conscience starts to surface. Will his haunted criminal past get the best of him?
In Stores!!

Ashland's mother, Bianca, fights hard to suppress the truth from her daughter because she doesn't want her to marry Jordan, the grandson of an ex-lover she loathes. Ashland soon finds out how cruel and vengeful her mother can be, but what price will Bianca pay for redemption?

In stores!!

243

Malcolm is a wealthy virgin who decides to conceal his wealth
From the world until he meets the right woman. His wealthy best
friend, Dexter, hides his wealth from no one. Malcolm struggles to
find love in an environment where vanity and materialism are
rampant, while Dexter is getting more than enough of his share of
women. Malcolm needs develop self-esteem and confidence to meet
the right woman and Dexter's confidence is borderline arrogance.
Will bad boys like Dexter continue to take women for a ride?
Or will nice guys like Malcolm continue to finish last?

In Stores!!!

What happens when a woman's devotion to her fiancee is tested weeks before she gets married? What if her fiancee is just hiding behind the veil of ministry to deceive her? Find out as Sean Mitchell takes you on a journey you'll never forget into the lives of Angelica, Titus and Aurelius.

Coming March 2008!!

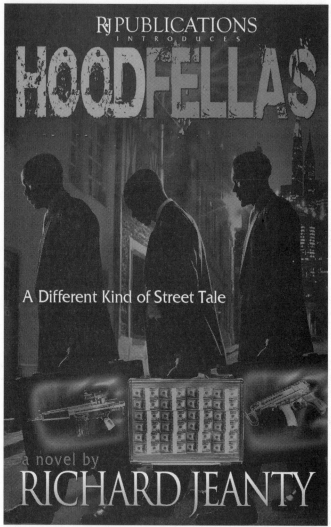

When an ex-con finds himself destitute and in dire need of the basic necessities after he's released from prison, he turns to what he knows best, crime, but at what cost? Who's gonna keep the neighborhood safe from his gang of thugs?

Coming November 2008

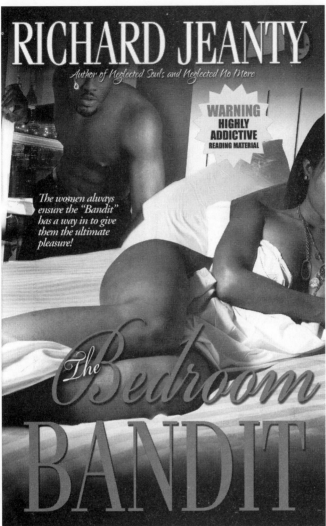

It may not be Wisteria Lane, but these desperate
housewives are fed up with their neglecting husbands.
Their sexual needs take precedence over the millions of
dollars that their husbands bring home every year. These
housewives a little TLC provided by the bedroom bandit.

Coming February 2009

PUBLICATIONS
BRINGING EXCITEMENT, FUN AND JOY TO READING

Use this coupon to order by mail

1. Neglected Souls, Richard Jeanty $14.95
2. Neglected No More, Richard Jeanty $14.95
3. Sexual Exploits of Nympho, Richard Jeanty $14.95
4. Meeting Ms. Right's Whip Appeal, Richard Jeanty $14.95
5. Me and Mrs. Jones, K.M Thompson ($14.95) Available
6. Chasin' Satisfaction, W.S Burkett ($14.95) Available
7. Extreme Circumstances, Cereka Cook ($14.95) Available
8. The Most Dangerous Gang In America, R. Jeanty $15.00
9. Sexual Exploits of a Nympho II, Richard Jeanty $15.00
10. Sexual Jeopardy, Richard Jeanty $14.95 Coming: 2/15/ 2008
11. Too Many Secrets, Too Many Lies, Sonya Sparks $15.00
12. Stick And Move, Shawn Black ($15.00) Coming 1/15/ 2008
13. Evil Side Of Money, Jeff Robertson $15.00
14. Cater To Her, W.S Burkett $15.00 Coming 3/30/ 2008
15. Blood of my Brother, Zoe & Ysuf Woods $15.00
16. Hoodfellas, Richard Jeanty $15.00 11/30/2008
17. The Bedroom Bandit, Richard Jeanty $15.00 January 2009

Name_____
Address_____
City_____State_____Zip Code_____

Please send the novels that I have circled above.

Shipping and Handling $1.99
Total Number of Books_____
Total Amount Due_____

This offer is subject to change without notice.

Send check or money order (no cash or CODs) to:
RJ Publications
290 Dune Street
Far Rockaway, NY 11691

For more info please call 718-471-2926, or visit www.rjpublications.com

Please allow 2-3 weeks for delivery

Use this coupon to order by mail

1. Neglected Souls, Richard Jeanty $14.95
2. Neglected No More, Richard Jeanty $14.95
3. Sexual Exploits of Nympho, Richard Jeanty $14.95
4. Meeting Ms. Right's Whip Appeal, Richard Jeanty $14.95
5. Me and Mrs. Jones, K.M Thompson ($14.95) Available
6. Chasin' Satisfaction, W.S Burkett ($14.95) Available
7. Extreme Circumstances, Cereka Cook ($14.95) Available
8. The Most Dangerous Gang In America, R. Jeanty $15.00
9. Sexual Exploits of a Nympho II, Richard Jeanty $15.00
10. Sexual Jeopardy, Richard Jeanty $14.95 Coming: 2/15/ 2008
11. Too Many Secrets, Too Many Lies, Sonya Sparks $15.00
12. Stick And Move, Shawn Black ($15.00) Coming 1/15/ 2008
13. Evil Side Of Money, Jeff Robertson $15.00
14. Cater To Her, W.S Burkett $15.00 Coming 3/30/ 2008
15. Blood of my Brother, Zoe & Ysuf Woods $15.00
16. Hoodfellas, Richard Jeanty $15.00 11/30/2008
17. The Bedroom Bandit, Richard Jeanty $15.00 January 2009

Name_____
Address_____
City_____State_____Zip Code_____

Please send the novels that I have circled above.

Shipping and Handling $1.99
Total Number of Books_____
Total Amount Due_____

This offer is subject to change without notice.

Send check or money order (no cash or CODs) to:
RJ Publications
290 Dune Street
Far Rockaway, NY 11691

For more info please call 718-471-2926, or visit www.rjpublications.com

Please allow 2-3 weeks for delivery

Use this coupon to order by mail

1. Neglected Souls, Richard Jeanty $14.95
2. Neglected No More, Richard Jeanty $14.95
3. Sexual Exploits of Nympho, Richard Jeanty $14.95
4. Meeting Ms. Right's Whip Appeal, Richard Jeanty $14.95
5. Me and Mrs. Jones, K.M Thompson ($14.95) Available
6. Chasin' Satisfaction, W.S Burkett ($14.95) Available
7. Extreme Circumstances, Cereka Cook ($14.95) Available
8. The Most Dangerous Gang In America, R. Jeanty $15.00
9. Sexual Exploits of a Nympho II, Richard Jeanty $15.00
10. Sexual Jeopardy, Richard Jeanty $14.95 Coming: 2/15/ 2008
11. Too Many Secrets, Too Many Lies, Sonya Sparks $15.00
12. Stick And Move, Shawn Black ($15.00) Coming 1/15/ 2008
13. Evil Side Of Money, Jeff Robertson $15.00
14. Cater To Her, W.S Burkett $15.00 Coming 3/30/ 2008
15. Blood of my Brother, Zoe & Ysuf Woods $15.00
16. Hoodfellas, Richard Jeanty $15.00 11/30/2008
17. The Bedroom Bandit, Richard Jeanty $15.00 January 2009

Name_____
Address_____
City_____State_____Zip Code_____

Please send the novels that I have circled above.

Shipping and Handling $1.99
Total Number of Books_____
Total Amount Due_____

This offer is subject to change without notice.

Send check or money order (no cash or CODs) to:
RJ Publications
290 Dune Street
Far Rockaway, NY 11691

For more info please call 718-471-2926, or visit www.rjpublications.com

Please allow 2-3 weeks for delivery

PUBLICATIONS
BRINGING EXCITEMENT, FUN AND JOY TO READING

Use this coupon to order by mail

1. Neglected Souls, Richard Jeanty $14.95
2. Neglected No More, Richard Jeanty $14.95
3. Sexual Exploits of Nympho, Richard Jeanty $14.95
4. Meeting Ms. Right's Whip Appeal, Richard Jeanty $14.95
5. Me and Mrs. Jones, K.M Thompson ($14.95) Available
6. Chasin' Satisfaction, W.S Burkett ($14.95) Available
7. Extreme Circumstances, Cereka Cook ($14.95) Available
8. The Most Dangerous Gang In America, R. Jeanty $15.00
9. Sexual Exploits of a Nympho II, Richard Jeanty $15.00
10. Sexual Jeopardy, Richard Jeanty $14.95 Coming: 2/15/ 2008
11. Too Many Secrets, Too Many Lies, Sonya Sparks $15.00
12. Stick And Move, Shawn Black ($15.00) Coming 1/15/ 2008
13. Evil Side Of Money, Jeff Robertson $15.00
14. Cater To Her, W.S Burkett $15.00 Coming 3/30/ 2008
15. Blood of my Brother, Zoe & Ysuf Woods $15.00
16. Hoodfellas, Richard Jeanty $15.00 11/30/2008
17. The Bedroom Bandit, Richard Jeanty $15.00 January 2009

Name_____
Address_____
City_____State____Zip Code_____

Please send the novels that I have circled above.

Shipping and Handling $1.99
Total Number of Books_____
Total Amount Due_____

This offer is subject to change without notice.

Send check or money order (no cash or CODs) to:
RJ Publications
290 Dune Street
Far Rockaway, NY 11691

For more info please call 718-471-2926, or visit www.rjpublications.com

Please allow 2-3 weeks for delivery

Use this coupon to order by mail

1. Neglected Souls, Richard Jeanty $14.95
2. Neglected No More, Richard Jeanty $14.95
3. Sexual Exploits of Nympho, Richard Jeanty $14.95
4. Meeting Ms. Right's Whip Appeal, Richard Jeanty $14.95
5. Me and Mrs. Jones, K.M Thompson ($14.95) Available
6. Chasin' Satisfaction, W.S Burkett ($14.95) Available
7. Extreme Circumstances, Cereka Cook ($14.95) Available
8. The Most Dangerous Gang In America, R. Jeanty $15.00
9. Sexual Exploits of a Nympho II, Richard Jeanty $15.00
10. Sexual Jeopardy, Richard Jeanty $14.95 Coming: 2/15/ 2008
11. Too Many Secrets, Too Many Lies, Sonya Sparks $15.00
12. Stick And Move, Shawn Black ($15.00) Coming 1/15/ 2008
13. Evil Side Of Money, Jeff Robertson $15.00
14. Cater To Her, W.S Burkett $15.00 Coming 3/30/ 2008
15. Blood of my Brother, Zoe & Ysuf Woods $15.00
16. Hoodfellas, Richard Jeanty $15.00 11/30/2008
17. The Bedroom Bandit, Richard Jeanty $15.00 January 2009

Name_____
Address_____
City_____State____Zip Code_____

Please send the novels that I have circled above.

Shipping and Handling $1.99
Total Number of Books_____
Total Amount Due_____

This offer is subject to change without notice.

Send check or money order (no cash or CODs) to:
RJ Publications
290 Dune Street
Far Rockaway, NY 11691

For more info please call 718-471-2926, or visit www.rjpublications.com

Please allow 2-3 weeks for delivery

PUBLICATIONS
BRINGING EXCITEMENT, FUN AND JOY TO READING

Use this coupon to order by mail

1. Neglected Souls, Richard Jeanty $14.95
2. Neglected No More, Richard Jeanty $14.95
3. Sexual Exploits of Nympho, Richard Jeanty $14.95
4. Meeting Ms. Right's Whip Appeal, Richard Jeanty $14.95
5. Me and Mrs. Jones, K.M Thompson ($14.95) Available
6. Chasin' Satisfaction, W.S Burkett ($14.95) Available
7. Extreme Circumstances, Cereka Cook ($14.95) Available
8. The Most Dangerous Gang In America, R. Jeanty $15.00
9. Sexual Exploits of a Nympho II, Richard Jeanty $15.00
10. Sexual Jeopardy, Richard Jeanty $14.95 Coming: 2/15/ 2008
11. Too Many Secrets, Too Many Lies, Sonya Sparks $15.00
12. Stick And Move, Shawn Black ($15.00) Coming 1/15/ 2008
13. Evil Side Of Money, Jeff Robertson $15.00
14. Cater To Her, W.S Burkett $15.00 Coming 3/30/ 2008
15. Blood of my Brother, Zoe & Ysuf Woods $15.00
16. Hoodfellas, Richard Jeanty $15.00 11/30/2008
17. The Bedroom Bandit, Richard Jeanty $15.00 January 2009

Name_____
Address_____
City_____State_____Zip Code_____

Please send the novels that I have circled above.

Shipping and Handling $1.99
Total Number of Books_____
Total Amount Due_____

This offer is subject to change without notice.

Send check or money order (no cash or CODs) to:
RJ Publications
290 Dune Street
Far Rockaway, NY 11691

For more info please call 718-471-2926, or visit www.rjpublications.com

Please allow 2-3 weeks for delivery

Use this coupon to order by mail

1. Neglected Souls, Richard Jeanty $14.95
2. Neglected No More, Richard Jeanty $14.95
3. Sexual Exploits of Nympho, Richard Jeanty $14.95
4. Meeting Ms. Right's Whip Appeal, Richard Jeanty $14.95
5. Me and Mrs. Jones, K.M Thompson ($14.95) Available
6. Chasin' Satisfaction, W.S Burkett ($14.95) Available
7. Extreme Circumstances, Cereka Cook ($14.95) Available
8. The Most Dangerous Gang In America, R. Jeanty $15.00
9. Sexual Exploits of a Nympho II, Richard Jeanty $15.00
10. Sexual Jeopardy, Richard Jeanty $14.95 Coming: 2/15/ 2008
11. Too Many Secrets, Too Many Lies, Sonya Sparks $15.00
12. Stick And Move, Shawn Black ($15.00) Coming 1/15/ 2008
13. Evil Side Of Money, Jeff Robertson $15.00
14. Cater To Her, W.S Burkett $15.00 Coming 3/30/ 2008
15. Blood of my Brother, Zoe & Ysuf Woods $15.00
16. Hoodfellas, Richard Jeanty $15.00 11/30/2008
17. The Bedroom Bandit, Richard Jeanty $15.00 January 2009

Name_____

Address_____

City_____State_____Zip Code_____

Please send the novels that I have circled above.

Shipping and Handling $1.99

Total Number of Books_____

Total Amount Due_____

This offer is subject to change without notice.

Send check or money order (no cash or CODs) to:
RJ Publications
290 Dune Street
Far Rockaway, NY 11691

For more info please call 718-471-2926, or visit www.rjpublications.com

Please allow 2-3 weeks for delivery

254

PUBLICATIONS
BRINGING EXCITEMENT, FUN AND JOY TO READING

Use this coupon to order by mail

1. Neglected Souls, Richard Jeanty $14.95
2. Neglected No More, Richard Jeanty $14.95
3. Sexual Exploits of Nympho, Richard Jeanty $14.95
4. Meeting Ms. Right's Whip Appeal, Richard Jeanty $14.95
5. Me and Mrs. Jones, K.M Thompson ($14.95) Available
6. Chasin' Satisfaction, W.S Burkett ($14.95) Available
7. Extreme Circumstances, Cereka Cook ($14.95) Available
8. The Most Dangerous Gang In America, R. Jeanty $15.00
9. Sexual Exploits of a Nympho II, Richard Jeanty $15.00
10. Sexual Jeopardy, Richard Jeanty $14.95 Coming: 2/15/ 2008
11. Too Many Secrets, Too Many Lies, Sonya Sparks $15.00
12. Stick And Move, Shawn Black ($15.00) Coming 1/15/ 2008
13. Evil Side Of Money, Jeff Robertson $15.00
14. Cater To Her, W.S Burkett $15.00 Coming 3/30/ 2008
15. Blood of my Brother, Zoe & Ysuf Woods $15.00
16. Hoodfellas, Richard Jeanty $15.00 11/30/2008
17. The Bedroom Bandit, Richard Jeanty $15.00 January 2009

Name_____
Address_____
City_____State_____Zip Code_____

Please send the novels that I have circled above.

Shipping and Handling $1.99
Total Number of Books_____
Total Amount Due_____

This offer is subject to change without notice.

Send check or money order (no cash or CODs) to:
RJ Publications
290 Dune Street
Far Rockaway, NY 11691

For more info please call 718-471-2926, or visit www.rjpublications.com

Please allow 2-3 weeks for delivery